ASSEMBLING HER TRUTH

NELSON FERGUSON

ASSEMBLING HER TRUTH

Written by

Nelson Ferguson

CITIOFBOOKS, INC.
3736 Eubank NE Suite A1
Albuquerque, NM 87111-3579
www.citiofbooks.com

Hotline: 1 (877) 389-2759
Fax: 1 (505) 930-7244

Ordering Information:

Quantity sales. Special discounts are available on quantity purchases by corporations, associations, and others. For details, contact the publisher at the address above.

Printed in the United States of America.

ISBN-13:   Softcover   979-8-89391-818-2
             eBook   979-8-89391-819-9

Library of Congress Control Number: 2025915232

FADE IN:

EXT. NEIGHBORHOOD - DAY

CHARLES, Caucasian, 19, skateboards on the sidewalk wearing a hood that covers half his face. He skates towards Carly's house.

EXT. CARLY'S HOUSE, FRONT PORCH - DAY

EMMA, Caucasian, Carly's mother, late 30's takes a huge set of flowers from a couple. She smiles and hugs them. She glances in the distance and sees Charles skating by.

As Charles approaches, he glances at Emma but quickly covers his face with his hood. He picks up his speed and skates past Carly's house.

Emma stares at Charles feeling concerned. She turns around and heads inside the house.

INT. CARLY HOUSE LIVING ROOM - DAY

Emma walks in carrying the flowers and places it on the table.

EXT. CHARLES'S HOUSE, DRIVEWAY - DAY

Charles slows down on his skateboard. He gets off and carries it.

INT. CHARLES'S HOUSE, LIVING ROOM - DAY - CONTINUOUS

Sarah, Caucasian, Charles's mother, late 30s, is looking at the monthly bill on the couch. She sighs.

The door opens.

Sarah looks up and sees Charles passes by as he heads upstairs without saying a word. She sighs feeling concerned for him.

INT. CHARLES'S HOUSE, CHARLES'S BEDROOM - DAY

Charles enters his room and closes the door softly. He puts his board down and sits at his desk. He wipes his tears from his eyes. He sees a missed called from Nate and a voicemail message

INT. MR. BATES PIZZA STATION - DAY - SAME TIME

NATE, Caucasian, friend of Charles, sits at a booth on the phone with his co-workers.

MR. BATES, Caucasian, walks up to his employees looking anxious.

> MR. BATES
> Have any of you heard back from
> Charles?

Nate takes his phone away from his ear as the co-workers look at each other anxiously and at Mr. Bates.

> NATE
> (sighs)
> No, we haven't.

Mr. Bates puts his head down feeling disappointed.

> NATE (CONT'D)
> But I think we should give him
> some space. He needs more time.

Mr. Bates softly nods his head with disappointment and slowly walks away as Nate watches him. Nate sighs heavily and goes back to work.

INT. CHARLES'S HOUSE, CHARLES'S BEDROOM - DAY

Charles still sitting at his desk looks at

the voicemail from his dad on his phone. He hesitates to press play. He gently hits the button and listens.

TONY, drug addict, late 30's, Charles's father, voice is heard.

                    TONY (V.O)
          Hey son, it me.

Charles sighs heavily.

                    TONY (V.O) (CONT'D)
          I know I'm probably the last
          person you want to talk to right
          now, but I heard the news about
          Carly.

Charles clenches his fist.

                    TONY (CONT'D)
          Just want to check in and see how
          you were doing.

Charles closes his eyes. He doesn't want to listen.

                    TONY (V.O) (CONT'D) (CONT'D)
          Um, feel free to call me back...

Charles quickly opens his eyes.

                    TONY (V.O) (CONT'D)
              (clears his throat)
          Or not. It's up to you if-

Charles quickly cuts off him off and deletes the voice message. He sighs and goes through his camera gallery of him and Carly.

INT. CHARLES'S HOUSE, HALLWAY - SAME TIME

Sarah's head is pressed against the door. She knocks on the door softly.

                    SARAH
               (softly)
          Charlie? Are you okay?

INT. CHARLES'S BEDROOM - SAME TIME

Charles ignores Sarah as he wipes his tears
while looking at pictures of him and Carly
looking very happy together on his phone.

INT. CHARLES'S HOUSE HALLWAY - DAY

Sarah is worried. She waits for Charles to
respond.

                    CHARLES (V.O)
               (softly)
          I want to be left alone mom.

Sarah takes her head away from the door and
sighs. She walks away giving him space.

INT. NORTHWOOD POLICE STATION, BERRY'S OFFICE
- DAY

DETECTIVE Berry, black, mid 40's, sits at his
desk as he stares at a beautiful photo of Carly
smiling.

A KNOCK on the door is heard.

Detective Berry looks up and sees the Deputy
Parker, black, late 40's.

                    DEPUTY PARKER
          Detective Berry? Kate Joseph is
          here.

                    DETECTIVE BERRY
          Thank you.

Detective Berry gets out of his chair and walks
out of the room.

INT. NORTHWOOD POLICE STATION, INTERROGATION
ROOM - SAME TIME

KATE, black, Carly's roommate, early 20's sits
at the table with her hands folded. She seems
very calm. She stares at herself through the
unidirectional perspective glass. A cup of hot
coffee rests beside her.

The door OPENS.

Detective Berry enters holding a manila
folder and closes the door. He looks at Kate
mysteriously.

                    DETECTIVE BERRY
          Thank you for coming Miss Joseph.
               (pauses)

          Glad that we were able to contact
          you before you left for your
          business trip to Europe.

Detective Berry sits down on the opposite side
of her.

Kate slowly nods her head.

Detective Berry opens the manila folder and
looks through the papers.

                    DETECTIVE BERRY (CONT'D)
               (sighs)
          I wanted to go over your statement
          that you told Northwood campus
          police. Just so I have a better
          understanding.
               (pauses)
          So you noticed Carly wasn't in the
          dorm around 10:30 p.m., correct?

                    KATE
               (nods her head)
          I do room checks on Thursday

nights.

Detective Berry slowly nods his head as if he's
impressed.

                    KATE (CONT'D)
          Residents have to be present
          around ten o'clock, so the deans
          know you were present there and
          you know alive.

Detective Berry nods his head with agreement.

                    DETECTIVE BERRY
          And after your shift, you noticed
          she was still missing?

                    KATE
          Yeah. Most residents who aren't
          there for room check have to
          check in at the front desk between
          eleven and four. Or else they get
          a memo violation from the dean.

                    DETECTIVE BERRY
          I get that, I talked to the deans.
          Is she normally there for room
          checks? Is she usually late?

                    KATE
          When I do my shifts she's there,
          but this was my first time seeing
          her gone. When I'm not working
          she's usually there.

                    DETECTIVE BERRY
          I see.
               (sighs)
          I checked your phone records the
          night of her death, you called her
          at 11:16 pm. Immediately, after
          your shift at eleven o'clock,
          correct?

Kate slowly nods her head "yes".

Detective Berry looks at the report concerned.

                    KATE
              (concerned)
          Is something wrong?

                    DETECTIVE BERRY
          In your statement you said you
          called her, but in your records,
          you called her boyfriend Charles
          at 11:06 p.m. Yes?

                    KATE
          Yes. I called him.

                    DETECTIVE BERRY
          Why call her boyfriend first
          instead of her?

Kate hesitates to answer. She quickly tries to
come up with an answer.

                    KATE
          I did call Charles, but he didn't
          answer. I thought I would give him
          a call to see if he was with him.

Detective Berry slowly nods his head.

EXT. NORTHWOOD POLICE STATION - DAY

Kate walks out of the station quickly. She
stops and takes out her phone. She looks at her
Facebook messages between her and Charles the
night of Carly's death.

On the chat, we see Kate's message sent to
Charles at 11:07

p.m. that reads: "Is Carly with you?"

Another message sent to Charles at 11:28 p.m.
that reads: "Answer my call! Carly is gone. Is
she with you?".

INT. CHARLES'S HOUSE, CHARLES'S BEDROOM - MORNING Charles is making up his bed.

The door OPENS and its Sarah.

                    SARAH
          (softly smiles)
     Hey. How are you doing?

Charles shrugs his shoulders while fixing his pillows.

Sarah looks down the hallway and looks back at him.

                    SARAH (CONT'D)
          (sighs)
     Um, Detective Berry is here again.
     He has more questions.

Charles stops fixing his pillows. He looks at his Sarah anxiously.

Detective Berry walks to the front of the door with Sarah.

                    DETECTIVE BERRY
     Good morning, Charles. I was
     wondering if we can talk again.

                    CHARLES
          (softly)
     Okay.

Charles slowly sits on his bed as Detective Berry walks in and sits at Charles's desk chair.

Sarah sits next to Charles for support.

As Detective Berry sits down and takes out his notepad from his briefcase.

                    DETECTIVE BERRY
          (sighs)
     So, I wanted to go over the
     questions I asked you about you

and Carly. Just so I have a better
understanding.

                    CHARLES
          (soft)
Okay.

                    DETECTIVE BERRY
You two were a couple in high
school?

                    CHARLES
          (softly)
Yeah, junior year. We were close
friends before.

                    DETECTIVE BERRY
Did you guys ever fight or have
problems between junior year and
the time she went to Northwood
College?

Charles puts his head down as Sarah feels
concerned for him.

                    SARAH
I'm sorry, but what does this have
to do with the investigation?

                    DETECTIVE BERRY
Ma'am, I'm just asking him a
simple question, and going through
their timeline.

                    CHARLES
          (softly)
No, we never fought and never
really encountered any problems.

Charles looks back up at Berry looking sorrowful.

                    DETECTIVE BERRY
     Never?

Charles softly shakes his head "no".

Detective Berry takes notes.

                    CHARLES
          Well, maybe not in high school but
          I guess when she started going to
          school.

                    DETECTIVE BERRY
               (looks up at Charles)
          At Northwood?

Charles softly nods his head.

                    CHARLES
          I think once she got there, I felt
          a little separated from her.

                    DETECTIVE BERRY
               (stops writing)
          What do you mean by that?

                    CHARLES
               (softly)
          I don't know, it felt like she
          wanted to hang out with other
          people than spend time with me.

Detective Berry nods his head slowly thinking
he can push Charles to spill more information.

                    DETECTIVE BERRY
          How'd that make you feel?

                    CHARLES
          Lonely I guess, I don't know. I
          think the people who she hanged
          out with kept her away from me.

Charlie twiddles with his hands.

                    DETECTIVE BERRY
          So you were jealous? You would
          say.

Charles is frustrated by Detective Berry's
remarks but remains his cool.

                    CHARLES
          (sighs)
Yeah. Maybe that's when it all
started when she decided to drink
behind my back. And started to
hang out with the wrong crowd.

                    DETECTIVE BERRY
Hung out with the wrong crowd? Do
you think her new friends put her
up to it?

                    CHARLES
          (softly)
Yeah, maybe but it could have been
anyone.

                    DETECTIVE BERRY
It's a strong possibility. I'm
planning to reinvestigate and talk
to new people on campus who knew
Carly.
          (pauses)
Would you say that's when Carly
started drinking or was this
before Northwood?

                    CHARLES
From what I know, yes.

                    DETECTIVE BERRY
Have you ever underage drink
Charles?

Charles and Sarah look at each other and back
at Detective Berry.

                    CHARLES
          (sighs heavily)
I've already told you, I don't. I
never will.

Sarah puts her hand on Charles's knee to calm

him down.

Charles looks at him angrily.

                    DETECTIVE BERRY
          (softly)
     Hey, hey. Charles? I need you to
     relax. Okay? I'm not trying to
     point fingers towards you.

Charles closes his eyes.

                    DETECTIVE BERRY (CONT'D)
     I'm trying to get to the truth
     and put together Carly's drinking
     incident. Figure out how a sweet
     girl like her would want to
     drinking.

Charles opens his eyes.

                    DETECTIVE BERRY (CONT'D)
                    (CONT'D)
     Along with where she got a fake
     ID.

Charles tries to calm himself.

                    SARAH
     Are there any updates on the bar?

                    DETECTIVE BERRY
     Yes. The bar has been permanently
     closed and the owner has lost his
     license.

Sarah sighs with relief.

                    DETECTIVE BERRY (CONT'D)
     I asked you this before, but I
     wanted to ask again. Have you ever
     encountered Carly drinking.

Charles looks down.

BEGIN FLASHBACK:

INT. CHARLES'S BEDROOM - NIGHT

Charles opens the door smiling with a bag of food in his hands. He looks down and sees an alcohol and throw up stain on the carpet.

A sponge on the floor with an alcohol stain.

He looks around the ground and sees an empty bottle of red wine is standing up.

CARLY, Caucasian, 19, Charles's girlfriend comes out of the bathroom wiping her tears with a vomit stain on her shirt.

She sniffles and breaks down.

                    CARLY
              (crying)
          Charlie, it's not what it looks
          like. I couldn't help myself-

Charles interrupts Carly looking at her seriously.

                    CHARLES
          This was the only weekend we had
          together, and this is what you do?
              (pauses)
          You go through my mom's wine
          cabinet-

Carly INTERRUPTS Charles.

                    CARLY
          Look I'm sorry. Okay, but I have a
          problem.

                    CHARLES
              (concerned)
          A problem? What problem?

                    CARLY
          I can call someone, rebuy the same
          wine. And your mother will never
          know-

Charles puts the bag of food on his desk. He walks quickly to Carly.

Carly takes a step back towards the wall feeling scared.

Charles lifts his hand, ready to slap her with anger but he stops himself when he sees Carly's face. He puts his hand down and tears up.

He picks up the sponge and pushes the sponge onto Carly's chest with force. He storms out of the room.

Carly breakdowns in tears. She goes down on her knees and scrubs the stain the carpet.

END OF FLASHBACK.

INT. CHARLES'S BEDROOM - MORNING (BACK TO PRESENT) Charles lifts his head up.

                    CHARLES
          No. I didn't know anything about
          her drinking problem.

Charles's hands sweat and shake.

Detective Berry notices Charles's hands tense up. He takes a note of it in his notebook and then closes it.

                    DETECTIVE BERRY
               (gets up)
          I think we're done here.

Charles sighs.

                    DETECTIVE BERRY (CONT'D)
          I informed Carly's mother Emma if
          we get anymore updates with the
          investigation.

                    SARAH
          Thank you.

                    DETECTIVE BERRY
               (to Charles)
          I respect your rights for not
          telling me if you were with Carly
          the night of her death.

                    CHARLES
          I wasn't with her.

                    DETECTIVE BERRY
          I keep giving you the chance to
          tell the truth Charles, but all
          I'm getting is just more lies.
          Your phone records show you were
          in the area that-

                    CHARLES
               (softly)
          If you're looking at me as a
          suspect, just say so.

Sarah looks at Charles concerned.

                    CHARLES (CONT'D) (CONT'D)
          Forget it, I want a lawyer.

Detective Berry looks at Charles vacantly. He
walks to the door about to leave but stops as
he opens the door.

                    DETECTIVE BERRY
          One more thing. Do you happen
          to know where Carly's satchel
          backpack is? It's not at her house
          nor her dorm room.

Charles shakes his head "no"

Detective Berry sighs and exits the room as
Sarah gets up and follows him.

INT. CHARLES'S HOUSE, HALLWAY - SAME TIME

Sarah closes Charles's door and catches up to

Detective Berry.

                    SARAH
     Is that it? Did you get everything
     that you need?

                    DETECTIVE BERRY
          (sighs)
     For now.

Sarah sighs heavily as she crosses her arms.

                    DETECTIVE BERRY (CONT'D)
     Looking at him, he's not doing
     well.

Detective Berry lets himself out.

Sarah walks back and opens Charles's door and
enters.

INT. CHARLES'S BEDROOM - SAME TIME

Charles's head is down, and his back is turned
away from his mom as he sits on his bed.

                    SARAH
          (softly)
     Hey, don't let Berry get to you
     like that. I'm going to head to
     work.

Charles turns his head back slowly.

                    CHARLES
          (softly)
     Bye.

Sarah puts her head down and leaves.

Charles stares at the area on floor where Carly
spilled her drink. He gets up and walks to
the closet. He opens the door and reaches for
something in the back corner.

He pulls out Carly's satchel backpack. He sighs

and looks at it intensely.

INT. MR. BATES PIZZA STATION - AFTERNOON

Charles enters looking very tired. He sighs softly.

Some of his co-workers see him. They walk up to him and hug him.

Mr. Bates step out of kitchen, and he is surprised when he sees Charles. He looks at Nate at the register.

Nate stares at Charles concerned.

                    MR. BATES
            (softly smiles)
        Thanks for bringing Charlie back
        to work.

                    NATE
        I didn't do anything. He came on
        his own.

Mr. Bates walks over to Charles.

                    MR. BATES
            (nods softly)
        Charles. Good to see you.

The co-workers stop hugging Charles, and they go back to work.

                    CHARLES
        Hi Mr. Bates.

                    MR. BATES
        Come. Let's chat.

INT. MR. BATES OFFICE - AFTERNOON

Charles sits in front of Mr. Bates's desk while Mr. Bates sits across from Charles.

                    MR. BATES
            (sighs)

How are you doing?

                    CHARLES
          (shrugs his shoulders)
     I'm okay. I guess.

                    MR. BATES
     You sure?

Charles nods his head softly with agreement.

                    MR. BATES (CONT'D)
     I'm so sorry for your loss kid.
     I know what it's like to lose
     someone you love.

                    CHARLES
          (puts his head down)
     Thanks.

                    MR. BATES
     Is there anything that I can do?
     Any way I can help?

                    CHARLES
          (softly)
     It's okay, but thanks.

                    MR. BATES
     I'm not sure how to say this but
     what are your plans?

Charles lifts up his head slowly.

                    MR. BATES (CONT'D)
     It's okay if you want to quit or
     manage some of your hours-

                    CHARLES
          (softly)
     There's no need to sir.

Mr. Bates adjusts himself on his chair.

                    CHARLES (CONT'D)
     Taking some time off of work and

                    spending time by myself has really
                    helped me deal with my grief.

Mr. Bates nods his head with agreement.

                         CHARLES (CONT'D)
                    As of now I'm comfortable coming
                    back here. I can't stay in my room
                    forever.

                         MR. BATES
                        (softly)
                    Okay.

                         CHARLES
                    But I appreciate you giving me
                    more time than I needed.

                         MR. BATES
                    You're welcome.

                         CHARLES
                    Also, for the time I was gone, I'm
                    willing to work extra hours than
                    before and-

                         MR. BATES
                        (concerned)
                    Charles, you don't have to do
                    that.

                         CHARLES
                    No, it's okay. Like I said I'm
                    comfortable now.

Charles softly smiles at Mr. Bates as Mr. Bates
smiles back.

INT. RETIREMENT HOME, LOBBY - AFTERNOON

Emma slowly types on the computer behind the
front desk.

A nurse looking through her purse walks to the
desk. She is in shock to see Emma.

                    NURSE
          Emma?
              (pauses)
          You're back so soon. I'm
          surprised.

                    EMMA
              (softly smiles)
          Me too.

                    NURSE
          How are you doing?

                    EMMA
              (sighs)
          I'm doing okay. Thanks for asking.

                    NURSE
          That's good. I won't keep you
          long, my friends are outside
          waiting. We're going out for
          lunch.

The nurse moves the clipboard closer to her and
signs out.

                    NURSE (CONT'D)
          I'll be back within the hour.

                    EMMA
              (smiles softly)
          Okay.

The nurse exits the building.

Emma watches the nurse leave through the front
glass doors as she walks to a red vehicle. Emma
stares at the red car.

BEGIN FLASHBACK:

EXT. CARLY'S HOUSE, DRIVEWAY - DAY

Emma and Carly laugh as they walk to the

front of the garage holding their hands with excitement.

                    EMMA
          Okay, I know you worked your ass
          off this school year. So, as an
          early graduation gift, I got you
          something.

                    CARLY
               (laughing and smiling)
          Oh my god. What did you buy?

                    EMMA
          Just wait.

Emma chuckles as she OPENS the garage door with the remote.

Carly's mouth drops in complete shock. She sees a new red car parked inside. She let's go of Emma's hand.

                    CARLY
               (scoffs)
          No freaking way.

Emma smiles with excitement.

                    CARLY (CONT'D)
          Mom, how?

                    EMMA
          Don't worry about that. What
          matters is that you earned it.

Carly smiles.

                    EMMA (CONT'D)
               (hands the keys to Carly)
          Congratulations.

Carly screams and laughs with excitement. She hugs Emma for a second and let's go.

                    CARLY
               (silly)
          Can I name her?

                    EMMA
               (laughing)
          Oh course. It's your freaking car.

Carly stares at the car with a smirk on her
face.

                    CARLY
          I'm thinking Betty.

                    EMMA
               (smiling at the car)
          Hello there, Betty.

Carly and Emma laugh and hug each other.

                    END FLASHBACK.

INT. RETIREMENT HOME, LOBBY - AFTERNOON

Emma watches the nurse getting inside the red
car with her friends. She stares at the car and
sheds a tear.

                    EMMA
               (softly to herself)
          Betty.

INT. MR. BATES PIZZA STATION - AFTERNOON

Charles steps out of Mr. Bates office. He walks
over to Nate at the booth.

                    CHARLES
               (softly)
          Hey.

                    NATE
               (hugs Charles)
          Hey. I'm assuming everything went

well in there?

                    CHARLES
It did, and I'm coming back.

                    NATE
Good.

Charles and Nate sit across from each other at
the booth.

                    NATE (CONT'D)
You look kind of pale. Does it
have to do with Carly?

Charles sits quietly and doesn't respond.

                    NATE (CONT'D)
Is it Berry?

                    CHARLES
      (sighs)
I don't even want to talk about
him.

                    NATE (concerned)
Why? What happened?

                    CHARLES
      (softly)
Nothing. It's just he's so nosy.

                    NATE
Nosy in what way?

                    CHARLES
I don't know. Stuff about Carly,
me, our relationship. It's like
leave me alone. Next thing you
know, he's gonna ask about our sex
life.

                    NATE
Charles-

                    CHARLES

How much do you want to bet that
he probably thinks that I forced
Carly into drinking?

                NATE
C'mon Charlie, don't think like
that. Okay? Berry is just doing
his job.

Charlie heavily sighs and gets up.

                CHARLES
I don't want to talk about this
anymore. I'm moving on but at this
rate I'm most likely to become a
person of interest.

Charles walks away.

Nate feels concerned for him.

INT. PET CLINIC, SARAH'S OFFICE - DAY

Sarah sits at her desk. She is holding a framed
picture of young Charles looking happy. She
takes her phone off her desk and decides to call
him.

EXT. MR. BATES PIZZA STATION, PARKING LOT - DAY

Charles opens the pizza delivery car trunk and
is about to put two boxes of pizza in it.

The VIBRATION of his cellphone is heard in his
pocket. He takes it out and answers.

                CHARLES
        (softly)
Hey mom. I can't talk right now,
I'm working.

                SARAH (V.O)
        (surprised)
Oh? You decided to go back?

                    CHARLES
          Yeah.

As Charles is about to close the trunk, he sees
a crumbled-up receipt of an old pizza order. He
picks it up and stares at it.

                    SARAH (V.O)
          Well, I just call and check on
          you. I want you to know that I'm
          here for you if-

                    CHARLES
               (breaks down)
          I-I have to go.

Charles hangs up the phone. He slams the trunk
and storms back inside the restaurant.

INT. MR. BATES PIZZA STATION - NIGHT

Mr. Bates looks at Charles cleaning a table
from his office window. He walks out and goes to
him.

                    MR. BATES
          Hey. Can we talk for a bit?

Charles stops cleaning.

                    CHARLES
               (softly)
          Okay.

Mr. Bates and Charles sit down at the booth.

                    MR. BATES
          I know you said you were fine about
          coming back to work, but I still
          feel concerned.

Charles puts his head down.

                    MR. BATES (CONT'D)
               (calm)
          Is there a reason why you

                    asked someone else to make the
                    deliveries today?

Charles slowly exhales.

                    MR. BATES (CONT'D)
               Charles, it's okay. I'm hear to
               listen not judge.

                    CHARLES
                 (softly)
               I found an old receipt in the
               truck earlier. I saw the address
               and the name and it was Carly's.

Mr. Bates folds his hands on the table.

                    CHARLES (CONT'D)
               I thought working today would
               help me move on but obviously my
               past of her keeps coming back. I
               apologize.

Nate comes out of the kitchen. He sees Charles
and Mr. Bates talking. He walks to them.

                    MR. BATES
               There's no need to.

                    NATE
               Uh, sorry to interrupt. Boss we
               got a order, but the address is in
               Emerald Fields.

                    MR. BATES
               Isn't that outside of town?

Nate nods his head with agreement.

                    CHARLES
               I can do it.

Nate and Mr. Bates look at each other and then
at Charles.

                    MR. BATES
          Are you sure?

                    NATE
          I can come if you want.

                    CHARLES
               (softly)
          No, it's fine, I'll go by myself.

Charles gets up and begins to get ready.

Mr. Bates and Nate watch Charles leave. They both look at each other concerned for him.

EXT. MR. BATES PIZZA STATION - NIGHT

Charles walks out of the restaurant carrying two boxes of pizza and puts the boxes in the trunk.

The pizza delivery car drives out of the parking lot.

INT. PIZZA DELIVERY CAR - NIGHT

As Charles drives, his hands sweat nervously. He rubs his hands on his work pants. He takes a deep breath and continues driving.

EXT. EMERALD FIELDS, NEIGHBORHOOD - NIGHT

Charles looks around as he is drives. He looks at the GPS indicating that he is close to his destination. He parks in front of a small but nice-looking guest house.

He stares at the house and sees the house is dark. He feels concerned.

EXT. DANIEL'S GUEST HOUSE, FRONT PORCH - SAME TIME

Charles walks to the front porch carrying the box of pizza. He rings the doorbell, but it doesn't make a noise. He presses it again but still doesn't make a sound.

He sighs heavily. He knocks on the door. He waits for a second, but no one comes to the door. He feels impatient and steps off the front porch.

INT. DANIEL'S GUEST HOUSE, BASEMENT - SAME TIME

DANIEL, Caucasian, tall, early 20s, paces back and forth.

                    DANIEL
              (yelling)
          You're being so dramatic. It's not
          a big deal!

NORA, Caucasian, 19, looks at Daniel furiously as she holds a pink blouse.

                    NORA
              (yelling)
          Not a big deal? I just found this
          in that room earlier today.

                    DANIEL
          It's obviously not mine. It's
          probably one of my cousins or-

                    NORA
              (throws blouse on the floor)
          Daniel, stop it.

                    (MORE)
                    NORA (CONT'D)
          I slept in that guest bedroom all
          the time. It wasn't there before.

Daniel INTERRUPTS Nora.

                    DANIEL
          Okay, then what are you implying?
          Hm?

Nora breathes heavily with anger.

                    DANIEL (CONT'D)
          (yelling)
     Say it!

                    NORA
          (yells)
     Are you seeing someone behind my
     back? Yes or no?

                    DANIEL
     No.

EXT. DANIEL'S GUEST HOUSE, BACKYARD - SAME TIME

Charles is bending down, watching Daniel and Nora argue through a small window. He feels a little nervous as the argument gets intense.

EXT. DANIEL'S GUEST HOUSE, DRIVEWAY - SAME TIME A car parks on the driveway.

PHILL, black, jock, early 20s, steps out of the car. He looks at the pizza delivery car. He looks around nervously.

INT. DANIEL'S GUEST HOUSE, BASEMENT - SAME TIME Nora crosses her arms.

                    NORA
          I leave for two weeks dealing with
          my family drama and now when I
          come back there's more.

EXT. DANIEL'S GUEST HOUSE, BACKYARD - SAME TIME

As Charles watches them argue, he looks around the room. Inside he sees a stool in front of white backdrop with photoshoot lights.

Phill walks to the backyard. He sees Charles peeking inside. He gets nervous.

                    PHILL
                  (yelling)
          Yo! What the heck man! Charles
          startles when he sees Phill.

                    CHARLES
          Shit.

Charles gets up with the box of pizza and runs.

Phill runs after him. He catches up and tackles
him on the ground. He puts Charles's arm behind
his back and grabs it tightly.

                    PHILL
                  (yelling)
          Stay down!

INT. DANIEL'S GUEST HOUSE, BASEMENT - SAME TIME

Daniel and Nora hear noise coming outside.
They look at each other concerned.

                    NORA
                  (looking out the window)
          Is that Phill?

Daniel and Nora get concerned and leave the
room.

EXT. DANIEL'S GUEST HOUSE, BACKYARD - SAME TIME

Phill shoves Charles's head in the ground.

                    CHARLES
                  (yelling)
          Let go of me!

                    PHILL
                  (yelling)
          Why the hell are you lurking on
          our property?

Charles struggles trying to break free.

Daniel and Nora enter. They see Phill hurting

Charles.

                    NORA
          Phill, stop.

                    DANIEL
            (to Phill)
          What the hell is going on?

                    PHILL
          This asshole was looking inside.

Probably watching you two.

Daniel looks at Charles.

                    DANIEL
          Dude, let go of him.

Phill gets off of Charles.

Charles coughs and tries to catch his breath.
He slowly gets and stares at Daniel, Nora and
Phill. He tries to make a run for it.

Daniel pulls on Charles's shirt and throws
him on the ground facing forward. He takes a
pocketknife from his pocket and points it near
Charlie's neck while pulling hair.

                    DANIEL (CONT'D)
          What the hell were you doing here
          kid?

                    CHARLES
            (panicking)
          I was here to deliver a pizza. I
          rang the doorbell and knocked, but
          no one answered.
            (catches his breath)
          So I came around back to get your
          guy's attention. I swear!

                    NORA
            (scoffs)
          Well, obviously you didn't.

Daniel puts the pocketknife to closer to Charles's face.

Charles tries to escape.

> DANIEL
> (whispers)
> I'm only going to tell you this once. Don't ever come back here again and never lurk on my property. Got it?

Daniel lets go of Charles's hair. He picks up the boxes of pizza and leaves as Nora throws tip money at Charles while he is on the ground.

Phill and Nora follow Daniel inside the house through the back.

Charles slowly gets back up. He looks at his arm and sees the bruise that Phill gave him. He looks at his uniform that is covered in grass stains and dirt.

He walks to the car and leaves Daniel's property.

INT. MR. BATES PIZZA STATION - LATER

Nate cleans the register. He sees Charles enter and notices his uniform covered in dirt. He is concerned.

> NATE
> (leaves the register)
> Dude, are you okay? What the hell happened?

Charles puts the car keys near the register and looks at Nate.

> CHARLES
> (softly)
> Tell Mr. Bates I quit. I can't do this anymore.

Charles walks out of the shop.

Nate watches him leave and feels bad.

INT. NORTHWOOD POLICE STATION, MALINOWSKI'S OFFICE - NIGHT

Detective Malinowski stands in front of his desk looking at a couple printed photos. He sees a picture of the damaged car in front of a tree.

He goes to the next photo and sees Carly's phone sealed in an evidence bag. He moves to the next photo and sighs heavily. He closes his eyes angrily.

INT. CHARLES'S BEDROOM - A WEEK LATER

Charles sits at his desk on his laptop.

Sarah KNOCKS on the door and opens it slowly.

                    SARAH
          Hey. You want to tell me what's
          going on with work?

                    CHARLES
              (softly)
          I quit.

                    SARAH
          How come?

                    CHARLES
          I can't move on from Carly.

Sarah walks to Charles and comforts him.

                    SARAH
          Should I stay home from work?

                    CHARLES
              (softly)
          No, it's fine. You go to work. I
          think I just need to be by myself.

Sarah stops comforting Charles and kisses his head. She stares and strokes his hair.

                    SARAH
          Hey, if you're interested, you can
          help me out at the pet clinic.

Charles softly smiles and thinks for a second.

                    CHARLES
          Actually, I would like that.

                    SARAH
          Good. I'll call my boss and tell
          her. We'll leave later today for
          my shift.

                    CHARLES
          Okay.

Sarah leaves the room.

INT. MR. BATES OFFICE - MORNING

Mr. Bates is sitting at his desk. He stares at a set of car keys that Charles turned in. He sighs and takes out a "HELP WANTED" sign from his desk drawer.

Nate walks to the door and knocks. He sees the sign that Mr. Bates is holding.

Mr. Bates stares at Nate.

                    NATE
          Don't do it. He'll come back.

Mr. Bates sighs heavily as Nate leaves. Mr. Bates's phone VIBRATES on his desk. He sees an incoming call from the Northwood Police Station and picks up.

INT. CARLY HOUSE, HALLWAY - MORNING

Emma stares inside Carly's room for a second and walks in.

INT. CARLY'S BEDROOM - SAME TIME

Emma looks around Carly's cleaned room with the bed made up and organized dresser. She sits down on the bed. She sees a framed photo of Carly and Charles inside a photo booth.

She takes out her phone from her pocket and makes a call.

INT. CHARLES'S BEDROOM - SAME TIME

Charles sits at his desk looking through Carly's notebook. He takes a look at her lecture notes. His phone VIBRATES on the desk. He sees it is Emma calling but ignores it.

He continues to look through Carly's notebook.

INT. CARLY'S BEDROOM - SAME TIME

Emma takes her phone away from her ear when Charles doesn't answer. She looks back at the photo of Carly and Charles.

INT. CHARLES'S BEDROOM - SAME TIME

As Charles flips to the next page of Carly's notebook, he makes it to a pocket shelf section. He sees a small, folded piece of paper sticking out.

He takes the paper from the pocket and Carly's school ID slips out. He picks it up and sees a dried smeared blood stain on it.

He stares at Carly's ID picture and feels anxious when he stares at the blood. He puts down the card and unfolds the piece of paper. He sees a reminder list that Carly wrote.

On the list it reads: "Return library book by Thursday" and "Get ID from 502 on Saturday"

Charles is confused. He stares at the number

"502" and looks back at the ID. He thinks for a second trying to put the pieces together on what it could mean.

INT. NORTHWOOD POLICE STATION, INTERROGATION ROOM - DAY Mr. Bates's hands are folded together as he sits at the table across from Detective Berry.

                    MR. BATES
          I never been concerned with
          Charles before. He's a great kid.
               (pauses)
          But he's been acting strange.

                    DETECTIVE BERRY
               (curious)
          Strange how?

                    MR. BATES
          He's been coming late to work and
          taking days off.

                    DETECTIVE BERRY
          Was this before or after Carly's
          death?

                    MR. BATES
          Before. I noticed this around mid-
          January.

Detective Berry writes down what Mr. Bates tells him on his notepad.

                    DETECTIVE BERRY
          Did you give him any warnings that
          he could lose his job for being
          tardy?

                    MR. BATES
          I did. He started to come back on
          time and then it happened again.

                    DETECTIVE BERRY

Was he working there, the night of
Carly's death?

                    MR. BATES
          (sighs)
No sir. He wasn't.

Detective Berry writes again in his notepad.

INT. PET CLINIC, SARAH'S OFFICE - DAY

With a blank look, Charles looks at the list
that Carly wrote, trying to figure out what
"502" means. He snaps out when he hears the
door opens.

He quickly puts the note in his pocket and sees
Sarah walking in with a baby dog in a small
cage.

                    SARAH
          I got our next patient.

Sarah chuckles. She looks at Charles and sees
that he is gloomy. She feels concerned.

                    SARAH (CONT'D)
          Everything okay?

Sarah puts the cage on the table near the
corner.

                    CHARLES
          (nods)
          Mhm. I'm fine. It's just I didn't
          think it would smell this, you
          know, bad.

                    SARAH
          (chuckles)
          You get used to it. Comes with the
          job.

The baby dog softly whimpers inside the cage.

CHARACTER: SARAH (CONT'D)
Aw. Want to come out little guy?

Sarah opens the cage and lets the dog out.

Charles softly smiles and walks to it. He and pets it and becomes gloomy again.

Sarah gets concerned when she notices Charles's reaction change from slightly happy to gloomy again. She pets the dog with him.

INT. MR. BATES PIZZA STATION - DAY

Nate hands a pizza box to a customer at the register.

Mr. Bates enters through the front door coming back from the police station. He sees Nate and walks to him.

MR. BATES
Hey, have you talked to Charles since he left?

NATE
No sir. I haven't.

Mr. Bates sighs.

MR. BATES
Maybe after your shift you should go talk to him?

NATE
(concerned)
I don't know if that's a good idea.

Mr. Bates gets upset. He crosses his arms while giving Nate an angry look.

INT. PET CLINIC, SARAH'S OFFICE - DAY Sarah washes her hands at the sink.

SARAH

See, that wasn't so bad. Right?

Charles closes the small cage door.

                    CHARLES
          He peed on me twice.

                    SARAH
          I told you it was going to happen.
          Maybe if you weren't so fidgety.

                    CHARLES
          I have ADHD. Sue me.

Sarah chuckles.

                    CHARLES (CONT'D)
          After today, I'm actually glad
          that I got the opportunity to help
          you. It makes me appreciate you
          more on how much work you put in
          while its just the two of us.

Sarah smiles proudly.

                    SARAH
          Thanks Charlie. It means a lot.

Sarah walks to Charles and hugs him. She stops
hugging him and grabs the small cage.

                    SARAH (CONT'D)
          I'll be back. In the meantime, you
          can clean up.

                    CHARLES
          Lord knows I need it.

INT. PET CLINIC, LOBBY - SAME TIME

Sarah exits the office carrying the small cage.

Charles looks down the hallway and sees Kate.
He is in shock and panics as he stares while
Sarah gives the dog cage to her.

BEGIN FLASHBACK:

INT. CHARLES'S BEDROOM - NIGHT

Charles's phone VIBRATES underneath his pillow as he is sleeps. He pulls it out and checks his notifications from Kate. He panics and quickly gets out of bed. He rushes out the door.

INT. CHARLES'S HOUSE LIVING ROOM - SAME TIME
Sarah is on the couch. She is sound asleep.

Charles slowly walks to the table in front of Sarah trying to not wake her up. He reaches Sarah's car keys in the key basket and slowly walks out the door.

END OF FLASHBACK.

INT. PET CLINIC, SARAH'S OFFICE - (BACK TO PRESENT DAY)

Charles continues to stare at Kate as Sarah talks to her. He tries to listen to their conversation. He moves away quickly from the door when Kate makes eye contact with him. He gets an incoming call from Nate but declines it.

EXT. CHARLES'S HOUSE, FRONT PORCH - EVENING

Nate is sitting on the footsteps waiting for Charles. He rubs his hands nervously. He stands up when he sees a car pulling up and on the driveway.

Charles and Sarah walk to him.

                    SARAH
              (surprised)
          Oh, hello Nate.

                    NATE
          Hi Mrs. Higgins.

Charles is confused as to why Nate is here.

                    NATE (CONT'D)
          I can't stay for long, but I
          wanted to talk to Charles.

Charles stares at Nate angerly not wanting to
talk.

INT. CHARLES'S BEDROOM - EVENING

Nate looks at the note Carly wrote.

Charles looks at the dried blood on Carly's
school ID. He places it on his desk in plain
sight.

                    NATE
          When did you find this?

                    CHARLES
          This morning. I've been trying to
          figure out what "502" means and-

                    NATE
          And?

                    CHARLES
          I'm not sure.

Nate folds the note and gives it back to
Charles. He thinks for a second. He looks at
Charles feeling concerned. He takes his keys
out of his pocket.

                    NATE
          C'mon, let's go.

                    CHARLES
          W-What? Where are we going?

                    NATE
          We're going for a drive. You need
          to relax.

INT. CARLY'S HOUSE, KITCHEN - NIGHT

Emma is on the phone as she holds a picture of
Carly.

                    EMMA
          Hi, Reverend Adams, how are you? I
          was meaning to call you last week,
          but I got a little busy.
               (softly laugh nervously)
          I was wondering if I could use the
          churches banquet hall for an event
          I'm planning.

Emma listens to the Reverend Adams on the other
end while looking at the picture of Carly.

INT. NORTHWOOD POLICE STATION, BERRY'S OFFICE
- NIGHT

Detective Berry sits at his desk on a phone
staring at a picture of Carly.

                    DETECTIVE BERRY
          I understand. This investigation
          is probably going to take a while.
               (pauses)
          I'll come on campus sometime this
          week to question more students.

The KNOCK on the door is heard.

Detective Berry looks up and sees the deputy.

                    DETECTIVE BERRY (CONT'D)
          Uh-huh. Here, I'll call you right
          back. Bye.

Detective Berry ends the call.

                    DETECTIVE BERRY (CONT'D)
                    (CONT'D)
          Come in.

The door opens.

DEPUTY JAMES, Caucasian, 42, hefty walks in looking concerned.

                    DEPUTY JAMES
          We heard back from our forensic
          team.

                    DETECTIVE BERRY
          And?

                    DEPUTY JAMES
          Traces of somebody else's blood
          were found.

Detective Berry slouches up and is concerned.

INT. NATE'S CAR - NIGHT

Nate drives on the road with Charles.

Charles rests his head on the window looking on his phone. He is looking at the Northwood University website page. He types the word "dormitories" in the search engine.

Charles clicks on the link for the girls' dormitories. He looks through the pictures displayed. He sees girls chilling in the lobby and other girls in their dorm rooms.

Nate takes his hand off the steering wheel and pats on Charles's shoulder.

                    NATE
          It's going to be okay bud.

Nate stops patting Charles's shoulder and puts it back on the wheel. He looks at Charles concerned. His phone rings and answers. He puts it on speaker phone.

                    NATE (CONT'D)
          Hey boss.

                    MR. BATES (V.O)
          Hey Nate. Did you talk to Charles?

Nate looks at Charles.

Charles gives Nate a serious look.

                    NATE
               (sighs)
          Yes, I have sir. Just give me at
          least three more days and he'll be
          back. I promise.

Nate ends the call and continues to drive.

                    NATE (CONT'D)
          You do plan on coming back right?

Charles looks at Nate and looks back at his
phone.

                    CHARLES
               (softly)
          We'll see.

Charles clicks on a link for the boys' dormitory
on Northwood campus. He scrolls and sees
pictures of the dorm lobby and dorm rooms on
how they look.

As Charles is scrolling down seeing more
pictures of the dormority, he scrolls to the
next picture and sees Daniel and Phill posing
outside them with the door opened.

He sits up as he recognizes them. He sees zooms
in and sees the number "502" on the door. His
eyes widen.

Nate looks at Charles concerned.

                    NATE
          Everything okay?

Charles shows the photo to Nate.

Nate is stunned. He gets nervous and continues driving as Charles breathes heavily as he stares back at the photo. He is annoyed.

INT. DANIEL'S GUEST HOUSE, GUEST ROOM - MORNING

Nora sits on the bed with her computer on her lap. She checks an article.

The title of the article reads: Female Student at Northwood University Dies in Drinking and Driving accident.

                    NORA
          (softly)
     Shit.

Nora swings her feet. She kicks an opened duffle bag filled with money is on the floor with a gun on top of it in front of her.

She scrolls down the page and sees a displayed picture of Carly smiling holding a dog in a pink blouse. She glances at Carly's outfit.

She bites her nail and stares Carly's photo. She recognizes the same blouse that she found. She stops biting her nail. She reads the article out loud.

                    NORA (CONT'D)
          (whispering)
     The 19-year-old college student
     was found dead alone on the side
     of the road. Alcohol was found in
     her system and was last seen at a
     near by bar.

Nora eyes widen.

                    NORA (CONT'D)
     After police searched her car,

                    and found a fake identification
                    card in her pocket. The nearby
                    bars security video shows that
                    the victim used it to gain entry
                    multiple times.

Nora looks very nervous.

                         NORA (CONT'D)
                    (whispering)
                    No way.

Nora hears heavy footsteps approaching. She
quickly closes her laptop.

Daniel and Phill enter the room.

Daniel sees Nora and kisses her forehead.

                         DANIEL
                    Hey beautiful. Still mad at me?

Nora doesn't respond.

                         PHILL
                    (to Nora)
                    Dan and I just talked a customer
                    earlier. Get this, he's willing to
                    pay triple if we get it done by
                    the end of today. He's on his way.

                         NORA
                    (annoyed)
                    I thought we were done doing this.
                    You know, taking a break.

                         PHILL
                    (laughs)
                    Well, breaks over.

                         DANIEL
                    (to Nora)
                    Are you okay?

                         NORA
                    Yeah. I'm fine.

Daniel and Phill look at each other concerned and leave Nora alone. They exit the room.

Nora opens her computer and continues reading the article.

INT. CHARLES'S HOUSE - MORNING

Charles quickly walks downstairs carrying his skateboard ready to leave.

The doorbell RINGS.

As Charles makes it down the stairs, he sees Detective Berry through the window. He takes a deep breath and opens the front door slightly.

                    DETECTIVE BERRY
              (smiling)
        Good morning, Charles.

Charles gives Detective Berry a stern look.

                    DETECTIVE BERRY (CONT'D)
        Do you mind if we talk?

Charles opens the door WIDER and lets him inside.

INT. DANIEL'S GUEST HOUSE, BASEMENT - MORNING
Nora quickly walks to Daniel and Phill.

                    NORA
              (raises her voice)
        Why didn't you guys tell me Carly?

Daniel and Phill look at each other concerned.

                    NORA (CONT'D)
              (yelling)
        The girl who died in the car
        accident.

She had a fake ID when the police found her. She went to Northwood.

                    PHILL
          We didn't know about-

Nora takes a gun from her back pocket and aims
it at Phill.

Daniel and Phill back up worried.

                    PHILL (CONT'D)
          (puts his hands up)
          Woah chill.

                    NORA
          (yelling)
          Stop gaslighting me!

                    DANIEL
          (reaching out his hands)
          Nora, put down the gun. Okay?
          We'll tell you everything.

Nora stops pointing the gun at Phill and
breathes heavily.

Daniel slowly walks to Nora. He slowly takes
the gun out of her hand and puts it in his back
pocket. He looks into Nora's eyes.

                    DANIEL (CONT'D)
          Don't aim a gun at someone unless
          you're planning to shoot.

Nora looks at Daniel furiously.

INT. CHARLES'S BEDROOM - MORNING

Charles sits at his desk looking at Detective
Berry with a blank face. He sighs as he massages
his head.

                    DETECTIVE BERRY
          I'm surprised by the news as you
          are.

Charles is nervous.

                    CHARLES
          I see.

                    DETECTIVE BERRY
          We don't know who's blood it is
          but we're making it a top priority
          with this new information.
               (pauses)
          I informed Emma last night and she
          wants answers.

Charles stays quiet and puts his head down.

Detective Berry is concerned.

                    DETECTIVE BERRY (CONT'D)
          Is your mom home? I know you're an
          adult now and I get the feeling
          since she was here the last time
          and-

                    CHARLES
               (softly)
          She's at work.

Detective Berry puts his hands in his pocket
and sighs.

He slightly glances towards Charles's desk and
sees Carly's bloody school ID. He looks back
at Charles suspiciously.

Charles looks up. He gets nervous when he sees
Detective Berry staring at his desk.

                    DETECTIVE BERRY
          I'm planning to reinvestigate more
          students at Northwood sometime
          this week. But I have to agree
          with you what you said before.
               (pauses)
          It's most likely Carly got the
          fake ID from someone there.

Charles slowly nods his head in agreement knowing what he now knows.

                    CHARLES
          (softly)
     Yeah.

Detective Berry's phone RINGS. He takes it out of his trench coat pocket and looks at it.

                    DETECTIVE BERRY
          (clears his throat)
     Excuse me.

Detective Berry walks away from the door and answers it.

As Detective Berry walks away, Charles looks at his desk trying to figure out what Detective Berry was looking at. He spots Carly's school ID.

Charles gulps. He slowly reaches for it while looking at Detective Berry on the phone in the corner with his back turned. He puts the ID in his pocket and sighs with relief.

Detective Berry turns back and comes back to the door.

                    DETECTIVE BERRY (CONT'D)
     Sorry about that but I have to get
     going.

Detective Berry looks down on Charles's desk. He notices Carly's school ID is gone. He gives Charles a serious look.

Charles gives him a serious look back as he watches Detective Berry leave the room. He opens his desk drawer and takes a box cutter knife. He gazes and examines at it intensely.

EXT. NEIGHBORHOOD - SAME TIME

Nate is inside his car. He is parked at the side of the road a few houses down from Charles's. He sees Detective Berry leave Charles's house and goes inside his car.

Nate watches Detective Berry leave looking through the rearview mirror.

EXT. CHARLES'S HOUSE - SAME TIME

Charles comes out of the house with his skateboard but in different clothing wearing a red and blue sports jacket, a cap, and dark sunglasses. He locks the door.

EXT. NEIGHBORHOOD - SAME

Nate sees Charles feeling concerned. He watches Charles skate the opposite direction that Detective Berry went. He turns on his car and follows Charles.

INT. DANIEL'S GUEST HOUSE BASEMENT - MORNING

Daniel, Nora and Phill are sitting together on the couch.

                    DANIEL
               (to Nora)
          Carly came to me asking for a fake
          ID.

                    NORA
          You don't know how to make them.

                    DANIEL
          I know. That's why I told her "No"
          since you were in the hospital and
          you're the only one who knows how
          to make them.

Nora crosses her arms.

                    DANIEL (CONT'D)
          (to Nora)
     She was willing to pay double the
     amount. So that's when Phill and I
     got greedy and made an ID without
     you knowing.

Nora angrily looks at Daniel breathing heavily.

                    PHILL
     After that, the three of us got
     close.

Daniel gives Phill an angry look.

                    PHILL (CONT'D)
          (looking at Daniel)
     Never mind.

                    NORA
     Are there any other IDs that you
     guys made without me knowing?

                    DANIEL
     No.

                    NORA
          (sighs)
     Where'd you guys put the camera
     equipment. Why is everything gone?

                    DANIEL
     It's stored in our dorm. I have
     family coming over soon so, Phill
     and I cleaned out the place.
          (pauses)
     Also, after the pizza guy showed
     up last week, it's best to keep it
     there for now.

                    NORA
     Good.

Nora looks at the white backdrop.

                    NORA (CONT'D)
          (points)
     What about that?

                    PHILL
          (to Daniel)
     We can take it down now if you
     have time.

Daniel looks at Nora concerned.

                    DANIEL
          (softly)
     Yeah. Let's go.

Nora crosses her arms and watches Daniel and
Phill intensely as they begin to dismantle the
backdrop.

INT. CHURCH, BANQUET HALL - MORNING

Emma looks around the empty banquet hall with
the reverend.

REVEREND ADAMS, 60s, Caucasian, puts his hands
in his pocket and smiles gracefully.

                    REVEREND ADAMS
     You made the right choice making
     this place for the memorial.

                    EMMA
          (nods her head softly)
     I feel like I needed to do this
     after the funeral.

Emma crosses her arms.

                    REVEREND ADAMS
     Do you need any help setting up? I
     can asks members around if they're
     free or-

Emma INTERRUPTS the reverend.

                    EMMA
              (softly)
       Don't worry. I have someone in
       mind who can help me.

Reverend Adams smiles and leaves.

Emma takes her phone out of her purse and calls
someone.

INT. PET CLINIC, LOBBY - SAME TIME

Sarah walks out of her office with a dog on a
leash giving it to a customer. The customer
takes the leash from Sarah.

                    CUSTOMER
       Thank you.

Sarah smiles and watches the customer leave.
Her phone VIBRATES in her pocket and takes
it out. She sees that it's Emma calling. She
answers.

                    SARAH
              (concerned)
        Emma?

EXT. NORTHWOOD UNIVERSITY SIDE GATE ENTRANCE
- MORNING

Charles still in disguised skates towards a
gated entrance.

He stops and looks at the Northwood University
monument sign. He looks through the gate.

Charles shakes the gate feeling how secure it
is. He takes a deep breath and looks at the
security camera looking at him. He looks away
from it nervously.

In the distance Detective Berry's car is parked
on the side of the road looking at Charles.

Charles looks in the distance and sees Detective Berry staring at him. He quickly turns his head and panics a little.

CHARLES
(softly to himself)
Remain calm, remain calm.

Charles takes a deep breath. He remembers that he's in disguise and thinks that Detective Berry doesn't know that its him. He looks around and sees a sign on the gates wall. The sign on the wall says: Swipe ID card to enter.

Charles looks at the scanner. He gets confused reading the sign and thinks. He starts to understand by what the sign means. He pats his pockets and takes out Carly's ID card.

He takes the ID and puts it up to the scanner.

The light TURNS green, and the gate OPENS slowly.

Charles looks back and sees that Detective Berry's car gone.

He takes a deep breath and walks inside.

Down the street, Nate in his car watching Charles enter the university.

EXT. NORTHWOOD UNIVERSITY – MORNING

As Charles enters the university, he sees students walking all over campus. He moves on the sidewalk when cars and people on golf carts pass by on the road.

Charles looks around confused. He realizes how big the university is. He turns around scared when someone touches his shoulder and he sees a tour guide.

                    TOUR GUIDE
          Hi, are you lost?

                    CHARLES
          Uh, pardon?

                    TOUR GUIDE
          Are you part of the campus tour?

The tour guide points to a group of people
inside a golf cart.

Charles plays along.

                    CHARLES
          Oh.
          (pauses)
Yeah, yeah, I'm part of the tour. So sorry, I
got lost.

                    TOUR GUIDE
          (laughs)
          It's okay. Northwood has a big
          campus, so I know the feeling.

The tour guide gives Charles a map of the
campus.

                    TOUR GUIDE (CONT'D)
          (smiling)
          Come on, we're just about to
          start.

                    CHARLES
          Uh, sure. Thanks.

The campus tour guide and Charles go inside the
golf cart with other people who are on the tour
and explore the university.

INT. PET CLINIC, SARAH'S OFFICE - MORNING

Emma is holding a framed photo of young Charles.

                    SARAH
          I think it's a great idea if
          Charles helps with Carly's
          memorial.
               (pauses)
          I don't see why he wouldn't.

                    EMMA
               (concerned)
          I've been trying to reach him
          after the funeral.

                    SARAH
               (softly)
          I'm really worried about him. He
          tells me fine, but I don't think
          that's the case.

                    EMMA
               (concerned)
          What you mean?

                    SARAH
               (sighs)
          I guess its a moms intuition
          feeling. He's been so quiet
          lately. Feels like he's still
          hurting with everything going on
          with Carly.

                    EMMA
          It takes time. Especially for
          someone young for his age.

                    SARAH
               (sighs)
          Yeah.

Emma comforts Sarah.

INT. DANIEL AND PHILL'S DORM ROOM - MORNING

Daniel is laying on his bed listening to music with his eyes closed.

Phill walks in. He looks down at the middle of the floor and sees the backdrop bag.

                    PHILL
          Dude, seriously?

Daniel doesn't respond.

Phill grabs his pillow from his bed.

                    PHILL (CONT'D)
               (throws pillow at Daniel)
          Dude!

Daniel takes off his headphones.

                    DANIEL
          What?

                    PHILL
               (sarcastic)
          Do you really think leaving the
          bag there on the floor is a good
          idea.

Daniel gets up from his bed and throws Phill's pillow back on his bed.

                    DANIEL
          Calm down. No one's going to look
          inside of it if they see it.

Daniel takes the backdrop bag and hides it under his bed.

                    PHILL
               (sighs)
          Sorry your right.
               (pauses)
          I'm just nervous man. I feel like

the police might come back to
campus.

                    DANIEL
          It's not like we have alcohol or
          fake ID's laying around.
               (pauses)
          I'm planning on taking the
          equipment and put it in storage.

                    PHILL
          Well, do it soon because people
          are talking.

                    DANIEL
               (curious)
          What are people saying?

Daniel's phone RINGS.

                    DANIEL (CONT'D)
          Hold on, I got to take this.

Daniel leaves the room.

INT. DANIEL'S GUEST HOUSE, BASEMENT - MORNING

Nora looks around, checking to see if Daniel
and Phill left anything important behind. As
she checks, she sees something sticking out
underneath the couch.

She gets on her knees and pulls it out. She
finds a white envelope. She opens it and sees
polaroid pictures. She takes them out and gasps
anxiously.

INT. NORTHWOOD UNIVERSITY SECURITY ROOM -
MORNING

One of the campus police officers and the chief
go to the security cameras.

                    CAMPUS OFFICER
          The card was accessed towards one
          of the gates accessed by Carly
          Walker at 10:34 a.m.

                        CHIEF
                    (confused)
          Isn't that the girl who was
          involved in the car accident that
          we recently reported?

The campus officer nods his head.

The chief and campus officer check the security
footage around 10:30 a.m. They see a man entering
the university in sunglasses and a cap.

                    CHIEF (CONT'D)
                  (concerned)
          We may have to put the campus on
          lockdown.

The campus officer gets worried.

INT. NATE'S CAR - MORNING

Nate circles around the gated university. He
follows a car in front of him.

The car in front of Nate goes to a gate that
leads to the men's dormitories and parking lot.
The person in front of him scans his Id card.

The gate OPENS.

Nate proceeds to follow the person in front of
him inside. He calls Charles but it goes to
voicemail.

                        NATE
          Hey Charles. It's me. Call me
          asap.

EXT. NORTHWOOD UNIVERSITY - MORNING

The campus tour is in front of the building talking about it in front of Charles and the people inside the golf cart.

> TOUR GUIDE
> (smiling and pointing)
> Over here, is the English
> department.

Students pursuing in journalism or writing get a good learning experience here at Northwood.

The people in the in the golf cart look amused.

As the tour guide continues to talk Charles hears yelling in the distance. He looks around and sees Daniel on the phone yelling at someone in front of a dorm entrance.

> DANIEL
> (yelling)
> No, you said you would pay triple.
> Okay?
> (pauses)
> Look I need more time, we're
> taking a break. A lot of stuff is
> happening on campus.
> (pauses)
> I'll explain later. Right now is
> not a good time. Bye.

Daniel hangs up the phone and goes inside the building.

Charles CLENCHES his fist. He takes off his sunglasses and gets off the golf cart and is about to follow Daniel.

The tour guide sees Charles about to leave.

                    TOUR GUIDE
          Excuse me, but no wandering until
          the tour is over.

Charles stops and tries to remain calm. He goes back inside the golf cart. While the campus tour guide isn't looking, Charles hesitates and leaves.

He goes up the hill to the dormitories.

EXT. NORTHWOOD UNIVERSITY MEN'S DORMITORY - SAME TIME

Charles walks to the entrance. He opens the door but its locked. He sees a scanner system at the side of the doors. He takes out Carly's ID and scans it.

The scanner denies his access.

Charles scans it again but the doors don't unlock. He gives up and walks away. He sees a boy pass by him and watches him go to the entrance.

The boy walks to the entrance. He scans his ID card to the scanner.

The door OPENS and the boy enters the building.

Charles quickly catches up to them and enters the building as well.

INT. MEN'S DORMITORY - MORNING

Charles looks around the building. He places his skateboard underneath a table. He sees Daniel talking to a group of people.

Charles slowly takes his box cutter knife of his pocket. He puts it up his jacket sleeve. He walks to him but gets startled when Nate grabs him by the shoulder.

                    NATE
          What the hell are you doing?

Charles gets angry he sees Nate.

                    CHARLES
          Leave me alone.

                    NATE
              (concerned)
          We shouldn't be here. We have to
          leave now.

Charles looks at Daniel.

Nate sees who Charles is looking at. He sees
Daniel.

                    NATE (CONT'D)
              (concerned)
          Charlie?

                    CHARLES
              (looking at Nate)
          I'm not leaving here until I get
          answers.

                    NATE
          We know nothing about this guy. We
          don't even know his name.

As Nate talks to him, Charles ignores Nate.
He sees Daniel leave his group of friends and
goes inside the elevator alone. He watches the
elevator go up and stop on the fifth floor.

Nate notices that Charles isn't paying attention
to him.

                    NATE (CONT'D)
              (raises his voice softly)
          Charlie!

Charles looks back at Nate.

                    NATE (CONT'D)
          Let's go. My car is outside.

Suddenly dorm resident's phones all PINGS at
the same time getting a text message in the
lobby.

Charles and Nate hear the noise. They look
around wondering what is going on.

Resident #1 and Resident #2 enter the lobby.
They walk past Charles and Nate.

                    RESIDENT #1
               (complaining)
          Ugh dude, I don't want to take
          this quiz today.

Resident #2 checks his phone.

                    RESIDENT #2
          May not have to, check your phone.
          It's an alert from the school,
          campus is on lockdown.

Resident #1 takes his phone out of his pocket.

                    RESIDENT #2
          (CONT'D) They're asking everyone
          to go in a building and to be on
          the lookout for a Caucasian man,
          wearing a red and blue sports
          jacket. Contact campus police if
          spotted.

Charles and Nate overhear Resident #1 and #2
talking.

Nate looks at Charles's outfit fitting the
description. He gets nervous and gives him a
serious look.

The sound of the elevator RINGS.

Charles rushes to the elevator.

                    NATE
            (runs after Charles)
        Wait Charles!

Charles gets inside the elevator and taps on the fifth floor alone.

The elevator door CLOSES.

Nate doesn't make it in time to the elevator and the doors close in front of him.

                    NATE (CONT'D)
            (to himself)
        Dammit.

Nates watches the elevator go up to see what floor Charles is going to. He sees it stop on the fifth floor. He takes the stairway and goes after him.

INT. MEN'S DORMITORY FIFTH FLOOR - MORNING

Charles gets off the elevator furiously. He walks around the fifth floor looking for Daniel. He peeks down the corner of the hall and sees Daniel walk out of his room shirtless in towel and flipflops.

Daniel leaves the door slightly open while he walks to a different corner of the hallway.

Charles quickly walks and goes inside Daniel's room.

INT. DANIEL AND PHILL'S DORM ROOM - SAME TIME

As Charles enters, he sees Phill sleeping on his bed. He gets anxious is about to leave but sees Daniel returning around the corner.

Charles hesitates and hides inside the closet cabinet.

Daniel comes back in the room. He gets his room key from off his desk and closes the door.

INT. MEN'S DORMITORY FIFTH FLOOR - SAME TIME

Nate enters the 5th floor from the stairway. He looks around panicking looking for Charles. He sees Daniel down the hall exiting his room.

INT. DANIEL AND PHILL'S DORM ROOM, CLOSET - SAME TIME

Charles opens the closet cabinet door slowly and watches Phill sleep. He takes a deep breath and slowly closes the cabinet door leaving it slightly opened.

Charles takes off his jacket. He puts on one of Phill's jackets but makes a little noise from the hangers.

Phill slowly wakes up. He looks around confused and hears movement. He looks at his closet suspiciously and gets up from his bed. He grabs a bat underneath his bed.

Charles peeks out and sees Phill slowly coming to the closet with a bat. He looks around and takes a spray bottle from the top shelf.

Phill OPENS the closet door.

Charles sprays Phill in the eyes as Phill screams and drops his bat. Charles pushes him on the ground and runs out of the room.

INT. MEN'S DORMITORY FIFTH FLOOR - SAME TIME

Nate hears noise down the hall. He gets concerned and sees Charles run out of the room coming towards him.

                    NATE
      What did you doCharles INTERRUPTS
      Nate.

                    CHARLES
            (hitting his shoulder)
      We got to go.

Charles and Nate leave the fifth floor through
the stairway.

Phill walks out of his room yelling in pain
rubbing his eyes.

                    PHILL
            (yelling)
      What the hell!

Phill tries to see but falls on the ground
losing his balance.

A couple of residents come out of their rooms
wondering what is going on.

INT. MEN'S DORMITORY LOBBY - MORNING

Charles and Nate come out of the stairway.

                    CHARLES
            (looking around)
      Okay, I think we're good.

                    NATE
            (sighs)
      You're freaking crazy.

Charles grabs his skateboard from under the
table.

Nate sees two security officers guarding both
exit doors.

                    NATE (CONT'D)
      We may have a problem.

Charles looks at the front exit and sees the guards.

                    NATE (CONT'D)
          Guess we're stuck here since
          they're looking for you.

Charles looks at the back exit. He sees Detective Berry talking to a two campus police officers near the door. He gets nervous when Detective Berry looks back at him.

                    CHARLES
          (to himself) Crap.

Detective Berry sees Charles and Nate. He walks to them.

                    DETECTIVE BERRY
          Afternoon gentlemen.

Charles and Nate both look at Detective Berry.

                    DETECTIVE BERRY (CONT'D)
             (puts hands in pockets)
          What are you boys doing here?
          Campus is on lockdown.

                    CHARLES
          Oh, we didn't know. I was just
          visiting my friend, Nate.
          Detective Berry looks at Nate.

                    DETECTIVE BERRY
             (to Nate)
          I thought you weren't interested
          in college.

Nate gets nervous.

                    DETECTIVE BERRY (CONT'D)
          You guys come with me.

Detective Berry escorts Charles and Nate outside going to the dormitory parking lot.

INT. PET CLINIC, SARAH'S OFFICE - MORNING Emma
shows Sarah pictures of young Carly.

                    SARAH
          (smiling)
     She's so pretty.

                    EMMA
          (smiling)
     She is.
     (pauses)
     Looking at back at these photos
     reminds me of how close we were
     while she grew up.

                    SARAH
     You two were always close?

                    EMMA
     Mhm. It's like we were sisters.

                    SARAH
          (sighs)
     Me and Charles are like that. With
     the two of us we're like best
     friends.

                    EMMA
     Can I ask you something?
          (pauses)
     Would you be mad if Charles kept
     secrets from you? Based on how
     close, you were.

Sarah sighs.

                    EMMA (CONT'D)
     Sorry, I only ask because Carly
     and I were close and since she
     didn't tell me about her drinking.

                    SARAH
          (softly)
     Yeah, I get it. Teens always

keep secrets from their parents.
Everyone has secrets.
          (pauses)
Not everything has to be shared.

Emma softly nods her head.

                    SARAH (CONT'D)
Would you be mad at Carly if she
did tell you about her drinking?
If she opened up about it?

Emma sighs and thinks.

INT. DETECTIVE BERRY'S CAR - MORNING

Detective Berry is driving with Charles. He
makes a phone call.

                    DETECTIVE BERRY
Hey, it's me. I'm calling to tell
you I spotted the suspect on
campus. He's with me now.
          (pauses)
No don't worry. I got it under
control. Thanks, bye.

Detective Berry ends the call. He looks at
Charles concerned.

Charles rests his head on the window annoyed.

                    DETECTIVE BERRY (CONT'D)
                    (CONT'D)
I didn't want to say in front of
your mother, but I know you've
been lying to me about Carly.

Charles remains silent.

                    DETECTIVE BERRY (CONT'D)
                    (CONT'D)
I get that your mom is trying to

> protect you, but she's not always
> to be there.

Charles looks out the window. He closes his eyes feeling guilty.

> DETECTIVE BERRY (CONT'D)
> (CONT'D)
> I'm going to take you in the station. We're going to need a blood sample. We're going to need a blood sample.

EXT. CHARLES'S HOUSE, DRIVEWAY - AFTERNOON
Detective Berry parks his car.

Charles exits the car and closes the door looking pissed off.

> DETECTIVE BERRY
> (rolling down the window)
> Mind if you give me Carly's school ID.

Charles takes out Carly's school ID out of his pocket and looks at it.

> CHARLES
> (softly)
> I know you saw it earlier.
> (pauses)
> To save you time, it's not my blood.

Charles gives the ID to him.

Detective Berry looks down at the card and back at Charles leaving feeling slightly relieved but still suspicious of him. He drives away.

Charles lifts his sleeve up and stares at the band aid. He stares in the distance watching Detective Berry leave.

INT. CHARLES'S BEDROOM - AFTERNOON

Charles enters lays on his bed. He gets a phone call from Nate but declines it. He sighs and rests his stares on at the floor.

BEGIN FLASHBACK:

EXT. TOWN, SIDE OF ROAD - NIGHT

Charles inside Sarah's car parks at the side of the road. He sees a bartender walk out of a bar checking his phone. He gets out of the car and quickly walks to the bar entrance.

The bartender gets suspicious when he sees Charles coming toward the bar. He sees how young he is.

>BAR TENDER
>>Hey, woah, woah, woah you can't go in there. This is a bar, not an arcade.

>CHARLES
>>I wasn't going inside.

>BAR TENDER
>>It looked like you were.

Charles sighs and pulls out his phone. He shows the bar tender a picture of Carly.

>CHARLES
>>Look, can you help me? Have you seen this girl? I think she's probably in there.

The bar tender seems to not care and doesn't bother look at the picture.

>BAR TENDER
>>Just leave kid, before I call security.

Charles sighs and puts his phone down. He looks inside the bar trying to see if he can spot Carly but doesn't. He walks away feeling defeated.

The bar tender looks at him as he walks away. He scoffs and continues to go on his phone.

As Charles quickly makes it back to his car, he glances at a brown bag near the edge of the sidewalk. He walks to it and as he gets closer, he sees that it's Carly's backpack.

He quickly walks to it and picks it up. He inspects it and he sees Carly's notebook. He looks back at the bar and back the bag. He gets inside his car and drives away.

The bar tender watches Charles leave.

END OF FLASHBACK.

INT. CHARLES'S BEDROOM - AFTERNOON

Charles's still laying on his bed sighs. His phone RINGS and he sees that it's Emma calling. He picks up.

                    CHARLES
          Hello?

INT. MR. BATES PIZZA STATION - AFTERNOON

Nate walks to Mr. Bates who is at the register.

                    NATE
          I'm sorry boss, but I feel like
          bringing Charles back seems
          impossible.

Mr. Bates puts his head down. He walks away from the register and goes to his office.

Nate breathes heavily.

INT. MEN'S DORMITORY, LOBBY - NIGHT

Nora is waiting in the lobby on the couch looking pissed off.

Phill walks out of the elevator. He walks past Nora.

Nora sees Phill.

                    NORA
          Hey, Phill.

Phill stops and sees Nora.

                    PHILL
          What's up?

                    NORA
          Are you okay? I heard something
          happened to you in the dorms
          earlier today.

                    PHILL
               (sighs)
          Some dude broke in our dorm. He
          sprayed something in my eyes.
          Luckily it didn't do directly in
          my eyes.

                    NORA
               (sighs)
          Have you seen Daniel?

                    PHILL
          He's trying to find a storage unit.
Haven't heard back from him.

                    NORA
               (gives Phill a note)
          Can you give him this?
               (pauses)
          When he comes back.

Phill gets concerned.

                    PHILL
          (takes the note from Nora)
     Alright.

                    NORA
     Thanks.

Nora leaves the building.

Phill unfolds the note and reads it.

INT. CARLY'S HOUSE, KITCHEN - NIGHT

Emma watering the flowers and plants she got
from her neighbors. She looks at a pile of
roses and touches them gently.

BEGIN FLASHBACK:

INT. RETIREMENT HOME - DAY

Emma is working at the front desk.

Carly enters the building holding a bouquet of
roses.

                    EMMA
     Ooh. Are these for me?

                    CARLY
          (laughing)
     No, Charles got it for me for our
     one year anniversary.

                    EMMA
     Awe, that's so sweet of him.

                    CARLY
          (smiling)
     I know, I love these roses,
     they're my favorite.

                    EMMA
               (smiling)
          You know, I have feeling that he's
          going to propose.

                    CARLY
               (scoffs)
          Mom, shut up.

                    EMMA
          What? With all the gifts he's
          giving you, I can tell that he
          really likes you.

                    CARLY
          Well, I doubt it.

Emma gives Carly smiles awkwardly and glances
away.

                    CARLY (CONT'D)
          You really think so?

                    EMMA
          Anything is possible.

Carly looks at Emma as if she's crazy.

END OF FLASHBACK.

INT. CARLY'S HOUSE, KITCHEN - NIGHT - BACK TO
PRESENT Emma stops touching the roses.

INT. CHARLES'S BEDROOM - NIGHT

Charles is on his phone. He goes on Carly's
Facebook and checks her friend list. He scrolls
down the list until he finds and recognizes
Daniel's account.

Once he finds it, he clicks on his profile.
He sees that his name is "Daniel Brunelle".
He looks at his bio and it displays that he
attends Northwood University.

Charles begins to glance at his page finding pictures of him and his friends. He feels disgusted and he throws his phone on his bed with anger. He picks up a hand mirror and slams it on the ground.

The glass scatters everywhere on the ground.

Charles closes his eyes and tries to calm down but can't. He thinks to himself for a moment and then he opens his eyes coming up with an idea. He grabs the phone from off his bed.

He logs out of his Facebook and creates a fake account. He signs up with the name "Carly Walker". He logs in with his new account and he searches Daniel's name in the search engine.

Charles CLICKS on "message" on his profile. He quickly types in the chat textbox. He stops typing and looks at his computer screen rereading what message he's going send.

The message reads: I know that you created the fake ID for Carly Walker. If you don't want the cops to find out meet me alone at Northwood Park tomorrow evening. Come alone.

He takes a deep breath and clicks on "send".

INT. DANIEL AND PHILL'S DORM ROOM - NIGHT

Phill is sitting on his bed re-reading the note Nora gave him.

Daniel opens the door and looks at Phill.

Phill gives Daniel a serious look.

                    DANIEL
              (confused)
          What's wrong?

Phill gives Daniel the note.

                    PHILL
          Nora's gone. She dropped out.

Daniel takes the note from Phill and beings reading it. As he is reading it, tears and anger build up in his eyes. He viciously throws the note on the ground.

                    PHILL (CONT'D)
          What the hell did you do?

Daniel's phone DINGS. He takes it out of his pocket and sees he has a received a new message from Facebook from "Carly Walker". He gets confused and opens the notification.

With Daniel's hand shaking, he reads the message to himself.

His eyes WIDEN.

                    PHILL (CONT'D)
          What's wrong?

Daniel breathes heavily with anger.

                    PHILL (CONT'D)
              (getting up from his bed)
          What is it? Is it Nora?

Phill walks to Daniel.

Daniel shows Phill the message he received.

                    PHILL (CONT'D)
              (grabs Daniel's phone)
          Wait is that real?

                    DANIEL
          Someone wants to be coward and
          hide behind Carly's name.

Daniel grabs his backpack from his bed and throws it at the window.

Phill rereads the message.

                    PHILL
          Why just you? Why not the rest of
          us?

Daniel POUNDS his fist on his desk.

                    PHILL (CONT'D)
          Do you think it's that guy who you
          were talking to earlier today?

                    DANIEL
          Probably, but why the hell would
          he threaten me?

Phill takes out his phone and makes a phone
call.

Daniel looks furiously out the window.

INT. DETECTIVE BERRY'S OFFICE - MORNING

Detective Berry is sitting at his desk drinking
in a glass cup.

The deputy knocks and enters.

                    DEPUTY JAMES
          We're still waiting on forensics
          on Carly's school ID that you
          found.
          (pauses)
          They noticed hat there's two
          different blood colors. One is
          lighter than the other.

Detective Berry puts down his glass and sighs.

                    DETECTIVE BERRY
          Come back when you have an update.

Deputy James nods and leaves.

INT. CHARLES'S BEDROOM - MORNING

Charles comes out of his bathroom. He looks at Daniel's replied message on his phone confirming to meet privately.

Nate enters knocks on the door. He sees a tape recorder on Charles's bed.

                    NATE
          (points to tape recorder)
     What's that for?

Charles looks at what Nate is pointing to on his bed.

                    CHARLES
     It's none of your business.

Nate sighs and gets concerned.

                    CHARLES (CONT'D)
          (annoyed)
     Can you leave? I'm not in the mood
     to talk.

                    NATE
     No. I'm not going anywhere.
          (pauses)
     Look Char-

Charles pushes Nate on the ground which makes him land on a piece of broken glass from the hand mirror he smashed.

Nate checks his arm. He sees the cut on his arm, and it starts to bleed. He looks back at Charles upset. He gets up and leaves.

Charles's phone RINGS on his bed. He sees its Emma calling again. He answers and puts her on speakerphone while he makes up his bed.

                    EMMA (V.O)
     Hey Charles. How are you? Hope I
     didn't call you at a bad time.

                    CHARLES
     No, it's okay. Not really doing
     anything.

                    EMMA (V.O)
     I was wondering if you're still
     wanting to help with Carly's
     memorial.

                    CHARLES
     Um, yeah, yeah. I am.

                    EMMA (V.O)
     Good. That was the purpose of
     calling. I wanted to see of you
     are available to come to the house
     this evening so we can plan.

Charles gets worried. He realizes that he is
supposed to meet Daniel around that time.

                    CHARLES
               (concerned)
     Uh, I don't think this evening
     would work for me. I'm going to be
     busy.

                    SARAH (V.O)
     Busy doing what?

Charles turns back and sees Sarah in front
of his door with her arms crossed. He gets
nervous.

Sarah gives Charles a serious look.

Charles looks away and looks at his phone.

                    CHARLES
               (to Emma)
     I'll be there.

Charles ends the call.

                         CHARLES (CONT'D)
                    (annoyed)
          I thought you left for work.

                         SARAH
          I was about to leave and then Nate
          came.
                    (pauses)
          He worried about you and I am too.

Sarah leaves looking upset and disappointed
that Charles is not speaking up.

Charles closes his eyes feeling stressed.

INT. DANIEL AND PHILL'S DORM ROOM - MORNING

Daniel quickly paces back and forth looking
very annoyed.

The door OPENS.

Phill enters the room.

                         DANIEL
                    (concerned)
          Well?

                    (pauses)
          Did you hear back from the guy?

                         PHILL
          No, he's not returning my calls or
          texts.

Daniel breathes furiously.

                         PHILL (CONT'D)
          What about you? Did you hear back
          from our cliens?

                         DANIEL
                    (shaking his head)
          No. I contacted everyone, and no
          one is answering.

Daniel sits on his bed feeling defeated.

                    PHILL
          Do you think Nora is behind this?

                    DANIEL
          No, it can't be her.

               (pauses)

                    (MORE)
                    DANIEL (CONT'D)
          But I find odd that as soon as
          she leaves town, this anonymous
          account wants to target me.

Daniel's phone PINGS on his bed.

                    PHILL
          Is that Nora?

Daniel reads a message on his phone.

                    DANIEL
               (grabbing the phone)
          No, it's the Carly account.
          They're asking to me at Northwood
          Park an hour earlier.

                    PHILL
               (sighs)
          Say "yes".

Daniel thinks for a moment. He types on his
phone and then locks it.

                    PHILL (CONT'D)
               (concerned)
          What'd you say?

                    DANIEL
          I agreed on the new time.

                    PHILL
          What the hell are you doing to do?

Daniel pauses and thinks for a second.

                         DANIEL
          I don't know, but I have a plan.

Phill looks at Daniel puzzled.

INT. GAS STATION - MORNING

Nora is at the register purchasing a bunch of snacks. She is wearing a Northwood University Hoodie.

As the cashier scans the items, Nora looks at her phone. She sees ten missed calls from Daniel. She unlocks her phone and blocks his number.

The door OPENS and its Detective Berry. He looks on one of the aisles and grabs a lighter.

Nora grabs the bag from the cashier.

                         NORA
          Thanks.

As Nora is about to head out, Detective Berry glances at Nora. He sees her wearing the Northwood University hoodie. He gets concerned.

                    DETECTIVE BERRY
          Excuse me, miss?

Nora stops and turns around to see Detective Berry. She gets nervous.

                         NORA
          Yes?

INT. CARLY'S HOUSE - MORNING

Emma answers the front door and sees Nate.

                         EMMA
                    (smiling)
          Oh my gosh, Nathan. It's been a
          while since I've seen you. How are
          you?

Nate tries to stay strong and not tear up. He shakes nervously while removes his hand from his arm. He shows the cut on his arm to Emma.

                    EMMA (CONT'D)
          My God, Nate are you okay?

Nate sheds a tear and doesn't say anything.

                    EMMA (CONT'D)
             (wrapping her arm around Nate)
          Here, come on. Let's go inside.

INT. GAS STATION - MORNING

Nora is looking down with her arms crossed. She feels guilty.

                    NORA
             (softly)
          I can't imagine what her mother
          and loved ones are going through.

Detective Berry looks at her concerned. He takes his card out of his pocket. He hands it to her.

                    DETECTIVE BERRY
          If you know anything else, you
          know where to reach me.

Nora looks up and takes the card from him. She stares at it.

                    NORA
          Will do.

Nora slowly walks away as Detective Berry watches her leave.

EXT. NORTHWOOD PARK - NIGHT

Charles is waiting on the bench. He takes out the tape recorder from his pocket and glances at it. He puts it back in his pocket.

Charles checks the time on his phone.

The time reads: 5:32 p.m.

Charles sighs with disappointment. He gets up and is about to leave. As he leaves, he hears the swing set swing back and forth. He turns around quickly and notices no one there.

Charles checks his surroundings. He walks to the swing set and stops it. As he turns around someone punches the side of his face making him fall on the ground.

Charles opens his eyes and sees Phill. He recognizes Phill's face from Daniel's guest house. He gets nervous.

Phill is shocked and then smirks at Charles.

                    PHILL
          (chuckles)
     Oh, it's you. Are you here to make
     pizza delievery?

Charles is a loss for words. He breathes heavily.

                    PHILL (CONT'D)
          (concerned)
     You sent that message to Daniel?
     Didn't you?

Charles CLENCHES his fists.

                    CHARLES
          (raises his voice)
     You guys killed her. You guys
     killed my freaking girlfriend.

Phill slowly walks closer to Charles. As he gets closer, he sees a couple walking towards them in the distance. He gets nervous thinking the couple seen him hurt Charles. He angerly looks back at Charles.

                    PHILL
            (serious)
        Get lost and keep your mouth
        shut... "Pizza boy"
            (pauses)
        Or else you'll end up just like
        Carly.

Phill stares back at the couple and walks away.

The couple walk in a different direction not noticing Charles on the ground.

Charles struggles to get up. He lays on his back and takes out his phone. He makes a call.

                    CHARLES
        Hi, Mrs. Walker.
            (softly groans)
        Yeah, I'm on my way, just going to
        be a few minutes late.

Charles ends the call and groans.

INT. DANIEL AND PHILL'S DORM ROOM - NIGHT

Daniel is on his bed looking at pictures of him and Nora on his phone. He keeps swiping and he sees a picture of him, his friend Oliver and Carly in the car taking a selfie together.

BEGIN FLASHBACK:

EXT. SIDE OF ROAD - NIGHT

People are exiting out of a building.

Daniel's inside his car parks at the side of the road in front of the building and waits. He looks over and sees drunk Carly at the end of the street trying to open a red car door.

Oliver, early 20's, Daniel's friend opens the door goes inside.

                    OLIVER
              (sighs)
          Thanks for picking me up.

Daniel ignores him and continues to stare at
Carly.

Oliver looks at what Daniel is staring at. He
sees Carly.

                    OLIVER (CONT'D)
              (scoffs)
          You wouldn't believe what she said
          in there.

Daniel gets concerned.

                    DANIEL
          I'll be back.

Daniel leaves his vehicle.

Oliver watches him go to Carly.

                    DANIEL (CONT'D)
          Everything okay?

                    CARLY
              (drunk, annoyed)
          No, my freaking keys are locked
          inside.

Carly continues to pull on the car door hoping
that it will open.

                    DANIEL
              (smirking)
          I can help if you want.

                    CARLY
          I don't need your help. Okay?

Daniel laughs. He smiles and stares at her ass
as she struggles opening the door. He gets
concerned when he sees blood on her pants in
between her legs.

                    DANIEL
               (scoffs)
          Not to be a bitch or anything,
          but I guess it's that time of the
          month.

Carly stops pulling in the door. She looks down
and sees her pants bleeding. She touches the
back of her pants. She nervously looks at the
blood on her fingers.

                    CARLY
          Shit.

Daniel laughs.

Carly takes her phone and keycard out of her
back pocket getting blood on it.

                    CARLY (CONT'D)
          My mom is going to kill me.

Daniel smiles and walks to Carly's car.

                    CARLY (CONT'D)
          Dan? What are you doing?

Daniel punches the car side window and the
glass SHATTERS.

As the glass shatters Carly drops her school
keycard. Daniel shakes the blood off his hand.

                    CARLY (CONT'D)
               (sarcastic)
          Great. Now my mom is really going
          to kill me.

                    DANIEL
          You're welcome.

Carly sighs and stares at her car for a moment.
She glances at the car.

                    CARLY
Wait, I-I don't think this is my
car.

                    DANIEL
          (confused)
Wait what?

                    CARLY
Shit. I forget Charles dropped me
off here,

                    DANIEL
Charles?

                    CARLY
Yeah, my boyfriend.

A dog barks loudly in the distance making Carly
looking towards that direction.

Daniel picks up Carly's school ID card with his
bloody hand without her noticing.

                    DANIEL
I'm guessing you ditched the AA
meeting.
          (pauses)
I can't imagine a drunk person
attend one. Unless your acting
trying to make a point.

                    CARLY
Well, I was sober when I went in.
Stayed there for like ten minutes
and then bailed.
          (pauses)
I got bored and decided to get
some beer at the store.

                    DANIEL
So, I assume the ID working, okay?

                    CARLY
               (smirking)
          Haven't been caught yet.

                    DANIEL
               (handing school ID to Carly)
          Want to hang out with us?

Daniel points to Oliver inside the car.

Carly grabs her ID from Daniel. She turns back
and sees Oliver staring at them.

                    CARLY
               (looks back at Daniel)
          Uh, no thanks. I-I'll just wait
          for Charles.

                    DANIEL
          Isn't he the one who brought you
          here? Don't you think he'll be
          upset if he saw you like this?

Carly sighs. She knows that Daniel is right but
somewhat feels scared.

                    DANIEL (CONT'D)
               (grabbing Carly's arm)
          Don't worry, nothing bad is going
          to happen while you're with us.

Carly gets nervous.

                    DANIEL (CONT'D)
               (pauses)
          Come on. You can text your so
          called "boyfriend" and tell him
          that you left with some new
          friends you met at the feeling.

Daniel and Carly walk together to Daniel's car.

END OF FLASHBACK.

INT. DANIEL AND PHILL'S DORM ROOM - NIGHT (BACK
TO PRESENT)

Daniel stops looking at the photos of him and
Carly. He hears the door open and close. He sees
that its Phill. He gets up looking concerned.

                    DANIEL
              (concerned)
        Well, what happened?

Phill walks to Daniel panicking and catching
his breath.

                    PHILL
        I may have messed up.

                    DANIEL
              (concerned)
        You were supposed to offer him a
        deal. How'd you mess up?

                    PHILL
        I know, but I just lost my temper
        and attacked him. I might've been
        seen hurting the guy.

Daniel furiously looks around pissed off at
Phill.

                    PHILL (CONT'D)
        They probably called the cops or
        checked on him. I don't know.
              (pauses)
        But I got good news. I recognized
        the person who's blackmailing us.

                    DANIEL
              (relieved)
        Who?

                    PHILL
        It's the pizza delivery guy. The
        dude who showed up at the house

last week. He's Carly's boyfriend.

Daniel thinks for a second. He remembers who Phill is talking about.

                    DANIEL
          (softly)
     Charles.

INT. CARLY'S HOUSE, LIVING ROOM - NIGHT

Emma walks with Charles inside the living room.

Charles sees Nate sitting on the couch with a bandage on his arm.

Nate and Charles look at each other furiously.

                    EMMA
     Nate was keeping me company today.
     He's going to help out in the
     memorial.

Emma's phone RINGS.

                    EMMA (CONT'D)
          (taking phone out of her
     pocket)
     Oh, I got to take this. Excuse me.

Emma leaves the room.

Charles sits next to Nate without saying a word.

Nate looks at Charles.

                    NATE
     Are you going to apologize?

Charles says nothing.

                    NATE (CONT'D)
          (concerned)
     I don't know what's gotten into
     you.
          (pauses)

(MORE)

NATE (CONT'D)
But I don't like this side of you.
You're becoming an ass. Charles
closes his eyes.

NATE (CONT'D)
Me, Mr. Bates, your mom is trying
to help and be there for you.

Charles opens his eyes. He feels bad.

NATE (CONT'D)
(touches Charles's shoulder)
If Carly was alive, do you think
she would want to see this side of
you.

CHARLES
(softly)
She already had.

Nate hugs Charles.

Emma comes back and sees Nate hugging Charles.

EMMA
(concerned)
Is everything okay?

NATE
(stops comforting Charles) Yeah,
everything is fine.

Emma looks at Charles concerned.

EMMA
Charles?

CHARLIE
(sniffles)
Yeah, everything is fine.

INT. NORTHWOOD POLICE STATION, BERRY'S OFFICE
- NIGHT

Detective Berry stares out window looking
outside. In the reflection, he sees the deputy
walks to the foot of the door and knock.

                    DEPUTY JAMES
          Got a minute?

Detective Berry turns around slowly.

                    DETECTIVE BERRY
          Any news on the ID?

                    DEPUTY
          The blood that was found on the ID
          matches the same person's blood
          that was found in Carly's car the
          night of her accident.
               (pauses)
          We know that it's not Charles's
          blood.

Detective Berry sighs with relief but feels
guilty for suspecting Charles. He puts his head
down and stares back out the window wondering
what to do now feeling stumped.

INT. DANIEL AND PHILL'S DORM ROOM - NIGHT Phill
is reading something on his phone.

Daniel enters the room.

                    PHILL
               (looking at Daniel)
          Got an email from the school.
          Northwood Police will be returning
          back to campus starting tomorrow
          in regards to Carly.

                    DANIEL
               (sighs)
          We leave before the dawn to go to

the storage unit.

Phill nods his head in agreement.

INT. CHARLES'S BEDROOM - NIGHT

Charles enters his room. He feels exhausted and goes on his phone. He checks out Daniel's Facebook page again through the fake account. He scrolls and he sees Daniel with Nora holding hands. He sees her tagged.

Charles recognizes Nora's face from the guest house. He clicks on her profile. He scrolls through Nora's page and sees a recent photo of her and Daniel kissing a month ago.

He looks at the caption that reads: Happy 2 years with this one with an emoji heart.

He scrolls through Nora's Facebook and sees more pictures of her and Daniel kissing and being comfortable with each other.

Charles clicks on "message". He types quickly and stops. He stares at his phone rereading what he's going to send.

The message reads: I know that Daniel cheated on you. I knowhe's the one behind the fake ID of Carly Walker.

Charles presses "send". He gets another incoming call from Tony. He sighs and stares at the call for a moment. He picks up and holds the phone up to his ear.

INT. MEN'S DORMITORY LOBBY - MORNING

Daniel and Phill are carrying the camera equipment and backdrop bag as they see the person at the front desk stare at them while they stare back.

Daniel and Phill walk outside to the dorm parking lot.

The person at the front desk watches them leave.

EXT. NORTHWOOD, CEMETERY - MORNING

Charles is sitting on the bench staring at Carly's grave. He moves the top of his skateboard with his feet.

Tony slowly walks to Charles with his hands in his pockets. He sits down next to him.

There is an awkward silence.

Tony looks at Charles concerned.

                    TONY
          (sighs)
     What did you want to talk about?
     Is it about Carly?

Charles puts his head down.

                    CHARLES
          (softly)
     Dad, I knew about Carly's
     drinking.
          (pauses)
     I tried helping her to quit, but I
     didn't do enough. I've failed her.

Tony sighs. He feels bad.

                    TONY
     The thing about addiction, it
     makes you feel self-absorbed, it
     creates this type of destruction.

Charles stays silent trying to understand.

                    TONY (CONT'D)
     To the point where people that
     care for the addict, affects them
     too.

Charles looks back at Carly's headstone.

                    TONY (CONT'D)
          Your mother tried helping me, but
          years later after I stopped with
          my addiction, I see why she made
          that choice.

Charles gets concerned. He is surprised what
Tony has said. His phone PINGS. He looks at his
phone and sees he received a message from Nora.

He reads the message from Nora says: You know
too much. Can we meet?

Tony sits closer to Charles, and he comforts
him.

INT. CHURCH BANQUET HALL - MORNING

People are setting up for the Carly's memorial.

Emma is on the phone.

                    EMMA
          It's okay.
               (pauses)
          No, no it's fine. Just call when
          you're on your way. Okay. Bye.

Emma hangs up the phone.

Nate carrying a box walks to Emma concerned.

                    NATE
          Is Charles coming?

                    EMMA
               (sighs)
          Yeah, he's just going to be late.

Nate sighs and walks away.

INT. MR. BATES PIZZA STATION - MORNING

Charles enters the pizza shop. He looks around
and sees Mr.

Bates cleaning a table. He walks to him.

Mr. Bates stops cleaning when he sees Charles.

                    MR. BATES
          Good to see you, Charles.

                    CHARLES
          You as well.
               (pauses)
          I'll be back soon.

                    MR. BATES
          (nodding his head)
          Take all the time you need.

Charles softly smiles.

Mr. Bates's phone RINGS. He takes it out of his
pocket and answers.

                    MR. BATES (CONT'D)
          Hello? Speaking?

Charles looks around with his hands in his
pockets.

                    MR. BATES (CONT'D)
          I'll be right there. Thanks. Bye.

Mr. Bates ends the call.

                    MR. BATES (CONT'D)
          Hey, can you watch the shop for
          me? There's a problem at the
          house.

                    CHARLES
          Sure.

Mr. Bates gives Charles the keys to the shop,
and he leaves.

Charles takes out his phone and re-reads the
message he sent to Nora asking to meet at Mr.
Bates Pizza Station. He looks out the window
and sees a taxi park in the parking lot.

Charles is concerned. He sees Nora get out of the car and walk towards the shop.

Nora enters the shop. She looks around and sees Charles. She recognizes him and walks to him.

> NORA
> You're behind the "Carly Walker" account?

Charles gets nods his head in agreement.

> NORA (CONT'D)
> (sighs)
> We a lot to talk about.

Charles gets concerned.

INT. STORAGE UNIT - MORNING

Daniel and Phill walk out of their storage unit.

Phill locks the door. He giggles the doorknob to make sure it's locked properly.

> PHILL
> Alright, I think we're good.

Daniel exhales heavily.

> DANIEL
> Yeah. I guess. We'll keep everything in there until the cops give up.

> PHILL
> What about this Charles guy? What are we going to do about him?

Daniel thinks for a second.

> DANIEL
> We know where he works. Let's go there.

Daniel and Phill walk away ready to head out.

INT. MR. BATES PIZZA STATION - MORNING

Charles is sitting at the booth across from Nora. His head is down now that he knows the truth about Carly and her fake ID.

Nora looks at Charles and she feels bad. She reaches inside her bag.

Charles looks up. He sees Nora takes out the pink blouse from her bag. He recognizes it. He slowly takes it from her and stares at it.

Nora reaches inside her bag again, and she takes out several polaroid photos out. She puts them on the table.

Charles leans forward dropping his mouth in awe surprised at what he sees. His body shakes nervously.

On the table shows photos of Carly tied up and passed out laying on the floor half naked in her bra and underwear.

Charles sheds a tear.

                    CHARLES
          D-Did he take these?

Nora takes out one more polaroid from her bag and shows it to Charles.

Charles sees Daniel kissing and posing with Carly half naked tied up. He takes the photo from Nora's hand and continues to cry.

                    NORA
          I've been thinking for a while,
          and I want to take accountability
          for what I did to her.

Charles sniffles.

                    NORA (CONT'D)
          On behalf of us, I'm sorry we
          killed her.

                    CHARLES
          It's not just you guys.
               (pauses)
          It's my fault too.

Nora sighs.

                    NORA
          Do you know where the restroom is?

                    CHARLES
          It's in the back.

Nora gets up and walks away slowly. She gives
Charles space.

Charles angrily looks back at the photos. He
stares at Daniel in the photo with Carly. He
looks out the window and sees a car quickly
come into the parking lot.

He slowly gets up holding the polaroid photo.
He sees Daniel and Phill step out of the car
and briskly walk towards the entrance. He gets
nervous.

Charles quickly grabs the photos. He puts them
in his jacket pocket and rushes to the kitchen
through the back exit.

EXT. MR. BATES PIZZA STATION, BACK ENTRANCE -
SAME TIME

Charles walks out the back entry way from the
kitchen. He breathes heavily and panics looking
around wondering what to do. He quickly takes
his phone out of his pocket ready to dial 911.

Suddenly, someone pushes Charles on the ground
making his phone break.

Charles looks up and sees Phill looking down on him. He quickly gets up ready to run but stops when Daniel comes around the corner.

Daniel and Phill slowly walk to Charles surrounding him on both sides.

Charles looks back and forth at them.

                    CHARLES
          (panics)
     What do you guys want?

Daniel and Phill look at each other.

                    DANIEL
     Come with us.

Charles is extremely nervous.

INT. MR. BATES PIZZA STATION - SAME TIME

Nora steps out of the bathroom. She looks around and sees Charles is missing. She quickly turns her head towards the window when the sound of a CAR SCREECH is heard outside.

She slowly walks to the window, and she sees Phills car exit the parking lot. She panics and breathes heavily. She thinks he kidnapped Charles.

She thinks and looks around wondering what to do. Suddenly, she checks her pockets and takes out Detective Berry's card that he gave her earlier in the gas station. She stares at it trying to catch her breath.

INT. DANIEL'S GUEST HOUSE, BASEMENT - MORNING

Charles is tied to a chair. He tries to remain calm as Phill tightens the rope.

Daniel steps out of a room holding a duffle bag. He stands infront of Charles.

Phill steps away and stands next to Daniel.

                    CHARLES
          What do you guys want from me?

                    DANIEL
          We want to make a deal with you.

Daniel drops the duffle bag. He bends down and unzips the bag.

As Daniels unzips the bag, he sees a large pool of money. He is in shock.

                    PHILL
          This money can all be yours if you
          stay quiet about our business.

Daniel stands up and kicks the bag towards Charles trying to attempt him to take the deal.

Charles stares at the bag and looks back at Daniel and Phill. He stares at them like they're crazy.

INT. MR. BATES PIZZA STATION - MORNING

A bunch of Northwood police cops are looking around.

Nora stands near the booth with Detective Berry and two other cops.

Detective Berry is writing on his notepad.

                    NORA
          I'm sorry for lying to you. I
          should've spoken up when I had the
          chance.

Detective Berry stops writing and sighs with anger. He looks at the other two officers with him.

Mr. Bates enters. He sees Detective Berry and walks to him.

                    MR. BATES
               (nervous)
          Have you found Charles?

                    DETECTIVE BERRY
          Not yet. We have officers in the
          area tracking Phills license plate
          now.

Officer #1 walks to Detective Berry.

                    OFFICER #1
          The campus is on lockdown, but
          officers have not found Daniel and
          Phill on campus nor at their
          homes.

Detective Berry looks at Nora suspiciously.

                    DETECTIVE BERRY
               (to Nora)
          Do you have any ideas where Daniel
          could have gone? Anywhere he could
          be hiding.

Nora sighs and thinks for a moment. An idea
comes to her head.

                    NORA
               (softly)
          I think I know where he is.

INT. DANIEL'S GUEST HOUSE, BASEMENT - MORNING

Charles sighs heavily still looking at the bag
filled with money.

Daniel behind Charles bends down. He looks at
the bag with him.

                    DANIEL
          There's more than ten thousand
          dollars in there.
               (pauses)

> It can all be yours, if you take
> the deal.

Charles stays quiet and thinks.

Phill crosses his arms.

                    CHARLES
          I don't want it.

                    DANIEL
              (chuckles softly)
          Of course, you want it.

Daniel looks at Charles's clothes.

                    DANIEL (CONT'D)
          Like look at you. No style,
          terrible sneakers. You're a slop.
              (pauses)
          Does your family not have enough
          to buy you decent clothing. Or is
          the pizza job not pay well. I'm
          guessing two dollars per hour?

This pisses off Charles. He breathes heavily.

                    CHARLES
          I know about the pictures you took
          of Carly.

Daniel is worried.

Phill is confused and gets concerned.

                    PHILL
          What the hell is talking about?

Daniel stays quiet.

Suddenly, the sound of POLICE SIRENS is heard
coming closer in the distance.

Daniel and Phill look at each other nervously.

EXT. DANIEL'S GUEST HOUSE - SAME TIME

Police cars swarm in front of the guest house.

Detective Berry comes out of the car with a bullhorn. He turns it on.

> DETECTIVE BERRY
> (speaks into microphone)
> Daniel Thomas? Phill Watson. We know that your inside bud. We know you have Charles.

INT. DANIEL'S GUEST HOUSE, BASEMENT - MORNING

Daniel breathes heavily as he aims his pocketknife towards Charles's neck. He looks up at Phill.

Phill looks at Daniel. He shakes his head "no".

Detective Berry's voice is heard from outside.

> DETECTIVE BERRY (O.S.)
> (speaks in microphone) We're giving you and Phill a minute to come out.

Daniel closes his eyes.

EXT. DANIEL'S GUEST HOUSE - SAME TIME

Detective Berry waits for Daniel and Phill. He's worried that they might hurt Charles. He looks down at Nora inside his police car in the back seat as Nora stares back at him nervously.

Other officers' steps out of the car looking at each other and then at Detective Berry.

Detective Berry stops looking at Nora and he gets an idea.

> DETECTIVE BERRY
> (speaks in microphone) We have your girlfriend, Nora in here in vehicle.

INT. DANIEL'S GUEST HOUSE BASEMENT - SAME TIME
Daniel and Phill look at each other.

Detective Malinowski's voice is heard from outside.

> DETECTIVE BERRY (O.S.)
> She admitted to making the fake ID
> for Carly.

Daniel closes his eyes tightly and sheds a tear. He feels bad and emotional when he hears Nora's name and that she's taking the blame for Carly's ID making when he knows it was him and Phill.

He stops himself and aims the pocketknife away from Charles's neck. He throws the pocketknife towards the corner and is about to walk out. Phill looks at him.

> PHILL
> Dude-

Daniel pushes Phill and walks upstairs.

Phill looks back at Charles. He feels some sort of guilt and follows Daniel.

Charles breathes heavily.

EXT. DANIEL'S GUEST HOUSE - SAME TIME

The police officers are impatient. They take out their weapons and walk to the house. As they get closer, they stop.

Daniel and Phill slowly step out of the house. They put their hands over their hands and surrender.

The officers go to Daniel and Phill. They forcefully pin them down on the grass as other officers go inside the house to get Charles.

As Daniel gets arrested, he looks up and sees

Detective Berry giving him a death stare.

INT. CHURCH BANQUET HALL - A WEEK LATER

People are dressed up nicely sitting and gathering for Carly's memorial.

In the front, a huge picture of Carly is displayed surrounded by lots of roses.

Reverend Adams and Emma are sitting in the front row while Sarah is sitting in the middle.

Charles is staring at Carly's displayed picture.

Nate walks to Charles.

                    NATE
          Hey. How are you holding up?

                    CHARLES
              (sighs)
          I think I'm okay. Just thankful to
          be alive.

Nate nods his head with agreement.

                    CHARLES (CONT'D)
          How's your arm?

                    NATE
          It's fine.

                    CHARLES
          I'm really sorry. I-

Nate INTERRUPTS Charles.

                    NATE
          It's alright.

Charles and Nate hug it out.

Reverend Adams looks at his watch and then at Emma. He tapes on her leg.

                    REVEREND ADAMS
              (whispering to Emma)
          I think it's a good time to start.

Emma looks back at the crowd. She gets up and
goes to the podium.

                    EMMA
          (smiling)
     Afternoon. I would like everyone
     to sit down. We're about to start.

The crowd settles down and take their seats.

Charles and Nate walk to the front row and sit
together.

                    EMMA (CONT'D)
     I want to thank everyone for
     coming. Along with volunteers for
     helping to set up for the service.
          (pauses)
     It's very appreciated. Charles and
     Nate smile at Emma.

                    EMMA (CONT'D)
     Before we begin, I like to say it
     means a lot that you're all here,
     not for me, but for Carly.

Emma sighs and tries to control her emotions.

                    EMMA (CONT'D)
     Just remember, that she's looking
     down on us right now.
     (pauses)
     Let's take this time today and
     acknowledge her, together.

Charles proudly smiles.

                    EMMA (CONT'D)
          (sighs)
     We'll start off with Charles who
     will begin with the remembrances.
     After him, if anyone would like to
     come and say a special memory of
     Carly feel free to do so.

                    (pauses)
               Charlie.

Emma goes back to her seat next to Reverend
Adams.

Charles takes a deep breath while Nate pats
on his hand on his shoulder. He walks to the
podium.

                    CHARLES
               (clearing his throat)
          Thank you, Ms. Baker.

Charles sighs. He stares at the crowd looking
at Sarah, Nate, and then at Mrs. Baker.

                    CHARLES (CONT'D)
               (slightly nervous)
          Sorry, um. I never spoke in front
          of this many people before.
               (pauses)
          Something I will always remember
          and never forget about Carly is
          how she made a positive impact on
          my life.

Emma softly smiles at Charles.

                    CHARLES (CONT'D)
          Her laugh, her honesty, everything
          about her changed my life by
          finding the happiness in my life
          through our friendship and while
          we dated.

Charles tries to hold back his tears.

                    CHARLES (CONT'D)
          Although, we may have had our
          downfalls here and there
               (pauses)
          Carly, I want you know that you
          changed my life in the best way

possible. Out of anyone, I'm glad
that it was you.

Charles stares at Carly's displayed picture
and then back at the crowd. He sees the crowd
tearing up and feeling emotional.

                CHARLES (CONT'D)
        Thank you.

Charles goes back to sit seat next to Nate.

Nate hugs Charles.

                REVEREND ADAMS
            (whispering)
        Are you okay?

Emma nods slowly.

                EMMA
            (sniffles)
        Yeah.

INT. CARLY'S HOUSE - NIGHT The doorbell RINGS.

Emma answers the door and sees Detective Berry.

                DETECTIVE BERRY
        Hello Emma.

                EMMA
            (smiling softly)
        Berry.

                DETECTIVE BERRY
        I know today was the memorial
        and I wanted to see how you were
        doing?

                EMMA
            (sighs)
        I'm okay.

Detective Berry softly nods.

                    DETECTIVE BERRY
          Goodnight, ma'am.

Detective Berry is about to leave.

                    EMMA
          Before you go, I want to thank
          you for helping with the
          investigation.

                    DETECTIVE BERRY
          Don't thank me, thank Charles.

Detective Berry leaves.

Emma sighs and closes the door.

INT. CHARLES'S BEDROOM - NIGHT

Sarah walks and looks around in Charles's
cleaned room. She sits on his bed and sees
framed photo of him and Carly on his nightstand.

She grabs it while turning on the lamp. She
stares at it on her lap.

BEGIN FLASHBACK:

INT. CHARLES'S HOUSE LIVING ROOM

Sarah is sitting on the couch. She stares at
Charles and Carly concerned.

Charles and Carly are standing in front of her.
They smile and they hold their hands.

Sarah sees them hold hands and looks back at
Charles.

                    SARAH
          She's pregnant, isn't she?

Carly smiles at Charles.

                    CHARLES
     No, mom.
          (pauses)
     Stop it.

Carly laughs softly.

                    CHARLES (CONT'D)
     I just wanted to let you meet my
     girl friend, Carly.
          (pauses)
     We've been going out for a while
     and felt like this was the right
     time.

Sarah smiles and looks at Carly. She scoffs
happily. She gets off the couch.

                    SARAH
     Girl friend?

                    CHARLES
     Yes, girl friend. That's what I
     just said.

Carly puts her head down and laughs. She looks
back up at Sarah.

                    SARAH
          (greeting Carly)
     It's so nice to meet you, Carly.

                    CARLY
          (smiling)
     It's nice to meet you as well.

Sarah and Carly hug each other and stop.

                    SARAH
          (laugh softly)
     Wow. It's just, you're so
     beautiful.

                    CARLY
               (laughs)
          Thank you.

                    SARAH
          Well, I'm happy for you two. Just
          hope I'm not a grandma if Charles
          proposes one day.

Carly laughs.

                    CHARLES
               (embarrassed)
          Mom, stop. Please.

Sarah looks at them smiling. She opens her arms
and hugs both of them at the same time.

END OF FLASHBACK.

INT. CHARLES'S BEDROOM - NIGHT (BACK TO PRESENT)

Sarah puts back the framed photo of Charles and
Carly on his nightstand. She sees something
inside of Charles's nightstand drawer that's
slightly opened.

As Sarah opens the drawer, she gasps as she
sees a ring box. She is shocked as she picks
it up and sees a silver ring. She puts the ring
back in the drawer.

Sarah turns off the lamp and gets up from off the
bed ready to leave the room. She looks back
at picture from the doorway one last time. She
smiles and closes the door.

INT. PRISON HALLWAY - NIGHT

A guard slowly walks down the hall with Daniel
holding him by the arms. The guard stops at the
phone booth with him.

                    GUARD
          Five minutes.

The guard uncuffs Daniel. He walks to the corner
and watches him intensely.

Daniel feels his risks. He breathes heavily
and closes his eyes. He picks up the phone and
dials a number.

INT. MR. BATES PIZZA STATION - NIGHT Nate is
near register cleaning the counter.

The restaurant phone at the counter RINGS.

Nate picks up it up.

                    NATE
          Welcome to Mr. Bates Pizza
          Station. How may I help you?

Nate pauses and listens to the person on the
line.

Charles comes out from the kitchen.

Nate turns back and sees Charles.

                    NATE (CONT'D)
          Charlie, someone is asking for
          you.

Charles gets confused. He takes the phone from
Nate.

                    CHARLES
          Hi this is Charles. Who am I
          speaking with?

                    DANIEL (V.O)
              (clears his throat)
          Um, hi Charles, it's me, Daniel.

Charles eyes WIDEN. He looks at Nate upset.

NATE
(whispering)
Who is it?

Charles is pissed.

CHARLES
(softly)
I don't feel like talking to you,
bye.

DANIEL (O.S)
No, wait, wait.

Charles ends the call.

Nate is concerned.

NATE
Who was it?

Charles walks away angrily.

INT. PRISON HALLWAY NIGHT

Daniel puts his head down feeling more guilty.
He puts the phone back on the retriever. He
stares at the floor with a blank face feeling
bad.

The guard walks to Daniel from behind and
handcuffs him.

INT. COURT ROOM - AFTERNOON

With a blank face, Daniel sits at the stand.

The JUDGE looks at Daniel angrily. He is
impatient.

JUDGE (O.S.)
Mr. Thomas, please answer Mrs.
Harris's questions.

Daniel looks up and stares at MRS. HARRIS,
black, 43, the prosecutor. He looks scared as
he stares at her.

Mrs. Harris steps forward to Daniel. She is impatient as well.

                    MRS. HARRIS
          Would you like me to repeat the
          question?

Daniel tries to focus. He nods his head slowly.

                    MRS. HARRIS (CONT'D)
          Were you with Carly Walker, the
          night of her death?

Daniel stays quiet for a second. He looks at his lawyer. He sighs and leans into the microphone.

                    DANIEL
               (softly)
          No.

                    MRS. HARRIS
          Remember Mr. Thomas, you are under
          oath.

Mrs. Harris can tell that Daniel is afraid. She knows that he is lying. She walks back and forth.

                    MRS. HARRIS (CONT'D)
          The Northwood Police Department
          has found traces of someone else's
          blood in the car the night of her
          accident.
               (pauses)
          The person's blood matches yours.

Daniel feels guilty. He knows he's screwed and can't get out of this one.

                    MRS. HARRIS (CONT'D)
          So, let me ask you again, were you
          with Carly Walker the night of her
          death?

Daniel begins to tear up. He looks at gallery

and he glance at Charles sitting with Nate and Sarah.

Charles angrily looks at Daniel.

Tony in the gallery on the opposite side looks at Charles concerned.

Daniel's closes his eyes.

                    DANIEL
          I was there, with her.

                    MRS. HARRIS
          And what happened?

Daniel lowers his head and closes his eyes. He breathes heavily ready to tell his truth.

BEGIN FLASHBACK:

INT. TOWN, SIDE OF ROAD - NIGHT

A car slowly parks at the side of the sidewalk. Nearby is small town shops and a local bar.

Daniel gets out of the passenger seat and closes the door.

The person in the car drives away.

Daniel checks his phone. He looks up and he sees Carly staring in the distance. He gets concerned and walks to her.

                    DANIEL
          Carly? Are you okay?

Daniel notices that Carly is drunk and tears on her face. He notices her holding her car keys.

Carly turns around to look at Daniel and she slightly falls and is about to pass out.

Daniel catches her and catches his balance as he holds onto her.

                    DANIEL (CONT'D)
          Woah, woah, woah. You're not okay.
          Here give me your keys, let me
          take you back on campus.

As they head to walk to Carly's car, from
behind, Carly's satchel backpack at the side
of the road.

INT. CARLY'S CAR, ROAD - NIGHT

Daniel is driving Carly's car on an empty road
surrounded by trees with drunk Carly. He at his
GPS on his phone.

Carly slowly wakes up and looks on the open
road. She sees Daniel is driving.

                    CARLY
               (confused)
          D-Daniel? Where are we?

                    DANIEL
          Relax, I'm taking you back to the
          dorm.

                    CARLY
          Where'd you find me?

Daniel ignores Carly's question as Carly pats
herself down searching for her phone.

Carly's phone VIBRATES. She looks and sees her
phone on Daniel's leg.

On her phone, we see missed calls from Kate and
Charles. She reaches for it, but Daniel pushes
her away.

                    CARLY (CONT'D)
               (annoyed)
          Give me my phone.

                    DANIEL
          Stop it. You'll get your phone

> back when you behave. You're still
> tipsy. Go back to sleep.

Carly looks out the window. She realizes that they are beyond outside of Northwood and is in the middle of nowhere stuck and trapped with Daniel.

She breathes softly as she waits for the right moment to grab her phone. She reaches for it again, but Daniel grabs her by the arm.

She gets up from her seat and tries to get her phone while Daniel tries to grab it out of her hand.

Daniel loses control of the wheel with Carly on top of him and blocking his view.

EXT. CARLY'S CAR, ROAD - SAME TIME

The car swarms and is out of control. It slightly moves side to side on the road.

INT. CARLY'S CAR, ROAD - SAME TIME Daniel raises his voice.

                    DANIEL
          Get off me, you witch.

Daniel tries to move Carly out of the way to see. He sees the coming to a tree. He opens his mouth in shock and closes his eyes.

BLACK SCREEN

The sound of the car crashing is heard.

EXT. SIDE OF ROAD - NIGHT

Daniel slowly wakes up and sees blood on him. He sees Carly's head bleeding. He sees the front window is shattered with the car hood smoking in a front of tree. He panics.

He slowly pushes Carly's body off his lap to the other side of the passenger seat. He unbuckles himself and gets outof the car. He leaves the door opened. He looks at the damage.

Carly slowly wakes up. She is alive.

Daniel sees Carly waking up. He slowly walks back to the opened car door.

Carly struggles to get up. She coughs up blood. She feels the blood on her hand. She looks up and sees Daniel. She is scared.

                    CARLY
              (weak)
         Ca- call for help.

Daniel angrily looks at Carly. He is pissed that she almost killed the both of them. He reaches inside and slowly picks Carly up onto the driver's seat.

Carly rests her head on the steering wheel. She is too weak to move.

Daniel still pissed at Carly, closes the front door and leaves the scene of the crime, leaving Carly to die.

END OF FLASHBACK.

INT. COURT ROOM - AFTERNOON Daniel still on the panel cries.

Mrs. Harris angrily looks at Daniel.

Daniel looks the gallery complaining and looking very angry. He looks at Charles.

Charles sheds a tear. He gets up and leaves the courtroom going to the lobby.

Sarah looks across the gallery and sees Tony.

She gets up and goes after Charles.

Tony gets up as well and follows Sarah.

The crowd and jury murmur.

Daniel puts his head down and closes his eyes as the judge BANGS his gavel with great force.

INT. COURTHOUSE, LOBBY - SAME TIME

Charles is on the floor curled up crying as Tony and Sarah walk to him and comfort him. They feel bad for Charles and cry together with him.

INT. CHARLES'S BEDROOM - NIGHT

A glass of water is beside Charles as he is sitting on his chair resting his head on the edge of his desk. He is still in shock after what happened.

Charles lifts up his head and takes a sip of water.

                    CARLY (O.S.)
          I hope that's water you're
          drinking.

Charles startles and sees Carly. In his imagination, he sees Carly leaning against the bedroom door. He starts to hallucinate.

                    CHARLES
          (softly)
          You're not real.

                    CARLY
          No, I'm not. I'm all in your head.

Carly steps away from the door and slightly sits on Charles's desk beside him.

                    CHARLES
              (sighs heavily)
     I want to kill him for what he did
     to you.

                    CARLY
     Is killing him justice to you?
     It's not going to bring me back.

                    CHARLES
     I'm so sorry for what he did to
     you.
              (pauses)
     But most of all, I'm sorry for
     failing you.

                    CARLY
              (puts her finger on Charles's
     lip)
     Shh. Don't ever let me hear
     you say you're sorry for what
     happened.

Charles softly cries as Carly comforts his
head holding it onto her chest.

                                   FADE OUT.